New Edge
Sword & Sorcery Magazine

VOLUME I, NUMBER 0 - MMXXII

New Edge Sword & Sorcery takes the genre's virtues—outsider protagonists, thrilling energy, wondrous weirdness, and a large body of classic tales—then alloys inclusivity, mutual creator support, a positive fan community, and enthusiastic promotion of new works into the mix.

Interior Illustrations

Gilead   @gileadtheartist

Hardeep Aujla   @hardeep.s.aujla

Carlos Castilho   'ho

Morgan King   ;ht

Aldo Ojeda   tus

Simon Underwood   _art

Remco Van Straten

David White

Staff

EDITOR   Oliver Brackenbury

DESIGN & LAYOUT   Nathaniel Webb

PROOFREADING   Jordan Douglas Smith

TRANSCRIPTION   Tania Morrison

COVER   Gilead

New Edge Sword & Sorcery is dedicated to making sure readers and creators from all walks of life have a seat at the table. Hate and harassment are not welcome here.

Letter from the Editor

Hello and welcome to this passion project, this experiment, this first ever issue of *New Edge Sword & Sorcery*! My name is Oliver Brackenbury, and I'll be your editor today.

This was unexpected for me even though, in early 2020, I did have vague thoughts about putting out a speculative fiction magazine. I'd just fallen in love with *Tales from the Magician's Skull* and decided to reach out to its editor for advice. Howard Andrew Jones, a real mensch, gave me an hour of his time over the phone. I soon realized a magazine wasn't something I was ready for, and put the idea aside.

In June of that year, I began serious work on my still untitled Sword & Sorcery novel, using a string of short stories to tell the tale of the adventuring life lived by a northern isle barbarian named Voe.

A year later, in 2021, I decided to launch my podcast, *So I'm Writing a Novel...*, as a way of building an audience for the book while I wrote it, alternating between behind-the-scenes craft-focused episodes following me writing the thing, and interviews with cool authors, editors, and publishers—mostly in the Sword & Sorcery scene.

After another year, in which I'd befriended many interesting people by interviewing them, and spending time in the Whetstone Tavern Discord, a conversation on the server about "how we get more young and diverse people into Sword & Sorcery?" began. An incredible energy was uncorked, sparking three straight days of intense discussion in which "New Edge Sword & Sorcery" was brought up as a possible term for a body of values, and rallying flag for a new wave of Sword & Sorcery popularity!

By June, some Tavern-goers were suggesting I do a New Edge Sword & Sorcery anthology. I thought about it, remembered what I'd called Howard about two years ago, then said, "How about a magazine? And would anybody want to help me put it together?"

The answer to both was a resounding "Yes!"

Since then, working almost entirely with other Whetstone Tavern patrons, I've been assembling issue #0 of *New Edge Sword & Sorcery*. It couldn't have happened without the Tavern, which I wouldn't have come to without the podcast, which wouldn't have happened if I wasn't writing that novel. It all seems so clear now as I type this, but it was a very organic evolution filled with unexpected turns.

I'm so happy it all went down the way it did. I've really enjoyed putting together a new Sword & Sorcery short fiction magazine! If enough people dig what we've put together here in issue #0 then we'll get to do more, likely by crowdfunding issues #1 and #2, benefitting from lessons learned and an actual budget to pay people.

I'd *love* that.

— *Oliver Brackenbury*

"If this is equality, I'll have none of it!"

The Curse of the Horsetail Banner

by Dariel R.A. Quiogue

Thick snow billowed and swirled across the white-cloaked steppe, driven by the moaning winds.

Orhan Timur halted his tired horse, cursing. Already the snowfall was so heavy he could no longer tell where the steppe ended and the mountains began. Soon he would not be able to see more than a few feet ahead. He was no longer even sure where he was. He strained every sense outward, desperately seeking any trace of the stag he had wounded at dawn.

Though some of his own wounds still seeped and men hunting him for his head could be anywhere, Orhan dared not give up his own hunt. He could not afford to. Game had been scarce and hard to find while he was on the run, and he hadn't eaten in three days. Without the food, winter would kill him as surely as any enemy sword.

The world was lost in a white haze. The cold wind dampened any scent of blood, and whatever traces there may have been, its gusts blew away. Nor could Orhan, despite his hunger-sharpened ears, hear anything but the ghostly moan of the wind across the vastness of the steppe. He blasphemed under his breath, snuffed the wind in vain one last time with a snarling grimace like a wolf or a big cat cheated of its prey, then kneed his horse into a circling walk, casting his strange hazel-gray gaze intensely upon the snow.

At last, with a sigh of relief he found deer sign: a tall tussock of dry grass spattered with dark blood. Beyond it, tracks in the snow. The storm had turned into an unlikely ally, for as the snow it deposited thickened, the heavy stag's prints grew deeper and took longer to obscure. And every few yards, there was more blood sign.

A little farther on he found the broken shaft of his arrow. He picked it up and cursed it. The thing was warped, and with the shifting wind the defect had prevented him from making a killing shot. The shaft must have broken and worked loose from the wound as the deer traveled, and in doing so it had restarted the bleeding. With blood and tracks to follow, Orhan pushed on.

Soon he was conscious of their passage over rising ground. As he had suspected, he had not been far from the mountains — but which ones? Was he in the foothills of the Drokpas to the south or east, or the haunted and forbidden Turuul range in the north? He had fled so far, dazed with weariness and wounds yet killing more than one stolen horse with his pace, that he was no longer sure where he was.

Just a few days ago, Orhan Timur would not have been riding to the hunt alone, but with a retinue of veteran guards and chosen companions, merrily passing around a skin of airag to warm their bellies. Among them would have been his blood-brother Jungar, khan of the western tribes, who every winter would ride to pay homage to Orhan, khan of the eastern tribes and Khagan, khan of khans, over the whole Murjen nation.

This winter, Jungar Khan had come not with gifts and his usual friendly jests, but with war. Not suspecting any treachery, Orhan had been caught with complete surprise.

Jungar. The mere thought of the name made Orhan's lips draw back in a savage snarl. *Jungar, my blood-brother, my anda, traitor and oathbreaker!* He had broken the most sacred bond known to the Murjen people, and now he was Khagan. *Not even in the deepest of the Nine Hells will you escape my vengeance*, Jungar, Orhan swore.

But first, I must have food.

For hours beyond his reckoning Orhan followed the blood trail, alternating between cursing

the stag for refusing to weaken and saluting it, even improvising a few verses in praise of its strength and stamina. Higher and higher up the mountain he followed, through a hidden pass he might never have discovered, then back down. As he crossed the pass, the snowfall ceased — and a great bawl of despair rang across the mountains, along with a terrible growling and snarling.

Orhan reined in with a curse.

A mere bowshot away rose a tall, rounded tumulus, and at its feet, a pack of wolves had fallen upon his stag and were even now tearing it apart. But the wolves had already been feasting even before the unfortunate stag had blundered into them. The flat space around the burial mound was strewn with human bodies.

Some were clad in the lamellar armor, pheasant-plumed helms and crimson scarves of the Wulong Empire's border cavalry, while most were in simple nomad herdsmen's coats and black fur caps. Orhan saw the skirmish had ramped a good distance from the mound, as mounted fights usually did, and some of the nomad bodies were almost at his horse's feet. Curiously, all the nomads wore all-black coats, a color the tribesmen normally avoided, and their caps bore a curious ornament: a pair of raven wings.

Orhan, suddenly realizing where he was with a surge of superstitious dread, wheeled his horse about and would have slammed heels to its flank to gallop away, snow-cloaked crevasses and slippery rocks be damned, for he was in the most forbidden of all sacred places to the steppe tribes.

The mound could only be the secret barrow of Toktengri, the first chieftain to ever call himself Khan of Khans in the days before the Murjen even had that name, and the dead nomad warriors were Khereyids, the fabled Raven Tribe who had been charged with the duty of preserving this site's taboo. It was death for any neither Khereyid nor of Toktengri's line, which was extinct, to ever set foot here.

But even as the horse turned, one of the Khereyid bodies moved and groaned. "Water," the Khereyid croaked, as harshly as the bird they were named for. "Please. One last drink of water."

Orhan halted the horse and wearily slid out of the saddle. He held his waterskin to the Khereyid's lips. The Raven was a young man, still utterly beardless, and upon seeing Orhan closely for the first time, gave a choked gasp.

"You! Not Khereyid," the dying man said. "Not supposed to be here... but not one of... them."

"I am Orhan Timur, lately of the Yesukai clan, now an outcast," Orhan said. "Who are 'they,' and what happened here?"

"Treachery! Black treachery! A Khereyid broke his sacred oath! Led... strangers here. Now — now we are cursed. Foreign dogs broke into the First Khagan's tomb... took his horsetail banner... now darkness will spread across the steppe...."

Orhan hissed in grim realization, recalling the last words of the legendary Toktengri Khan. 'Bury me seated, my banner of victory in hand, looking down upon our eternal enemy to the east. Do this, and my spirit shall keep our lands forever free of the rice-eaters' cities. But fail to keep my tomb inviolate, and I swear wolves and ravens shall fill the land like black clouds and devour all life within it.'

"Where did they go?" Orhan demanded.

"East," the youth whispered. "But beware! They have — " his last breath came in a rattle then he was still.

Orhan Timur closed the dead youth's eyes then turned a burning gray gaze east. The victory-bringing banner of Toktengri,

found! No tribesman of the steppes would ever rest knowing that sacred relic was in foreigners' hands. A darker, wilder thought had also come unbidden and unexpected to him, filling his heart and guts with fire; what tribesman of the steppe would not rally to the chief who possessed the banner?

In his mind's eye, he saw a vision of the tribes riding at his back, a great black horsetail banner dancing above their heads as they ran down the broken remnants of Jungar's broken host, singing as they slew. "Toktengri, you will provide me with the weapon I need to unseat Jungar and take my khaganate back," Orhan whispered.

He refilled his near-empty quiver from the Khereyids', appropriated a horn archer's thumb ring to replace the one he'd lost in the battle with Jungar, then remounted and turned his horse's head east.

Wolf howls split the moonlit night from north, south, and west.

Orhan slitted his catlike eyes in concern. It seemed wolf packs were converging from all across the steppe, scores of shadowy shapes loping behind him and to either side, while wolf tracks all but obliterated the trail of the cavalcade he followed. It was unnatural for wolves to gather in such numbers in winter, even more unnatural for different packs to run so closely together without fighting. It could only be the magic of Toktengri's banner. The curse was real.

And the wolves behind were gaining upon him.

Orhan counted his arrows, counted the nearest wolves, listened to his horse's heavy breathing as it kept a steady pace across the snows, trying to gauge how far he dared to push it. But it was driven now as much by fear as his will to keep going. On through

the night it ran, as tired and hungry as its rider, unable to stop for even a mouthful of snow to slake its thirst. Nor did Orhan dare to slake his own burning need for nourishment by drinking of the horse's blood as he'd been taught as a child, for he needed it to keep all its energy. Only a steppe horse could have borne such a punishing pace for so long.

They passed dead horses and men, and when the wolves devouring them turned upon him and his mount, Orhan shot them. He wished he could have retrieved those arrows, but dared not stop.

The men were Wulongan soldiers by their armor, and by the hacked-up wolf bodies strewn around them Orhan saw they had died hard. Their horses must have collapsed from exhaustion, burdened by the weight of men in heavy scale armor — and ill-gotten gold. For the dead horses' saddlebags and the men's clothes, torn up by the wolves, had spilled cups and bangles, dishes and ewers, jewelry for a hundred brides, all of gold.

Orhan smiled grimly. Would that Toktengri's curse worked only in this simple manner!

But it did not. Only a few wolves had stayed to feast on the carcasses. Contrary to their nature, more had kept running in relentless pursuit of the tomb robbers. At least the harsh steppe winter and the wolves were steadily thinning the enemy for him. But how many would he have to face when he caught them?

He tried to recall previous battles, the daredevil raids he'd made with the barest handful of men, the fox's tricks he'd used when outnumbered, to find a plan he could reuse or adapt. But exhaustion and hunger made thinking hard. He closed his eyes, trying to will the dull ache away.

He jerked awake to a pandemonium of barking, baying, and

the unmistakable screeches of an eagle in distress.

Dawn had snuck up on him as he slept, painting the eastern sky with a soft wash of purple, salmon and gold. The trail he'd been following was nowhere in sight. Instead, before him was a hunter's yurt, ominously innocent of the usual morning fire's smoke. Dark shapes in torn rags littered the snow, dark stains beneath them. And a sextet of wolves were leaping and snapping around a man-high oaken branch set in the ground, harrying the great golden eagle whose jesses were still tied to the perch.

Orhan would have ridden on, desperate to find the trail again. He turned his mount's head away. The eagle screamed, shrill and defiant, knowing no surrender. It was a kindred spirit on the lonely, enemy-haunted steppe.

With a snarl Orhan kicked the horse into a gallop for the camp. He shot two wolves before they were even aware of him, then he was among them, his scimitar licking out, not at any wolf, but at the rawhide tether.

The freed eagle shot skyward. The remaining wolves surrounded Orhan's rearing and plunging horse, the horse so panicked that all Orhan's skill with the scimitar was near useless. While one wolf menaced the horse's throat, another danced and circled behind it, preparing to fall upon its hind legs.

A tawny streak flashed past Orhan's head, and the wolf behind his horse yelped in pain. The eagle had clawed its face, blinding it in one eye.

Orhan at last got the mount under control. He charged the wolf before him, swerving aside and leaning down at the last moment to sweep his blade across its neck. The horse trampled another with lashing forehooves. He looked for the remaining two wolves.

They were no longer attack-ing him. Instead, they were run-ning in confused circles, the eagle swooping down at them then climbing away in a breathtaking aerial dance. Orhan dropped the scimitar to dangle from his wrist by its sword knot, whipped his bow back out of its case and feathered the last wolves.

To his surprise, the eagle cir-cled low about him until he put out his arm, upon which the rap-tor settled.

"Your master has gone to the Four Winds," he told the bird gently, removing its jesses. "You should go now. You're free."

But the eagle did not go. Orhan regarded the bird closely. It was a male, he now saw, but an unusually large one, of a race that generations of steppe falcon-ers had bred for hunting wolves. "Have the gods sent you to aid me? Or was it the spirit of Tok-tengri that bade you stay? Either way, my thanks. You were as good as a hundred arrows, my brother. I shall rename you for that — Zunjebei, Hundred Arrows."

The eagle whistled and ruf-fled its wings. Orhan followed its gaze and discovered one of the bodies around the yurt was still moving.

A young man, in the black khalat and ravens wing-decorated hat of the Khereyid. The young man's eyes were pleading, as if he desperately wanted to tell Orhan something. Orhan dismounted and knelt beside the dying war-rior.

"Who are you, and what is your tale?" Orhan asked roughly. For this Khereyid was all too likely the traitor who'd led for-eigners to Toktengri's tomb.

"Turgudai. I am — I was Khereyid. But I betrayed my tribe. I wanted her," he gestured at the body of a young woman. The youth's face was waxen from loss of blood, but sheer determi-nation gave him the energy to speak. "Khaliun, daughter of the eagle hunter Kush Beg. She re-fused me, I guessed because I am poor as all Khereyids are, for we cannot raise large herds in those mountains. I was mad for her. For her bride price, I thought to plunder the tomb of Toktengri Khan."

"You should die slowly," Orhan growled, standing up. There were a thousand ways he could think of to make the traitor suffer for his crime, but there was no time for most of them. He be-gan to draw his scimitar, meaning to eviscerate the man and leave him bleeding.

"Wait! Listen! Kill me only after you have heard what I must say. Khaliun made me realize what a great wrong I had done. I cannot make amends for my crime now. But for whatever it's worth, I have a warning and a gift for you.

"Beware the Wulongan leader, Lao Cheng! He is a eu-nuch, but no fat idler – he is a sorcerer and a sword master. Also, take the vial inside my robe. It's a potion by Lao Cheng, it will renew the vigor of man or horse no matter how tired or hungry. With it you can catch up with them before they reach the bor-der forts."

The youth closed his eyes. "I am ready to accept my fate now."

"Tell Toktengri's spirit I shall retrieve his banner," said Orhan. He took the vial, then drew his scimitar and hewed off Turgu-dai's head.

Finding the trail again proved easier than Orhan had feared.

Daybreak had brought un-mistakable signs that had been absent at night, in the form of great flocks of carrion birds, mostly ravens. The first flocks he saw led him toward emptied win-ter camps, their residents either fled or devoured by wolves. Then he saw the black river in the sky that swirled and eddied, but trended in a near straight line east.

He spurred his mount toward it at a gallop, the potion Turgudai had given him having put new fire in its veins. His own empty stomach still ached dully, but he was alert and clear-headed again, the pain of his wounds forgotten, his grip on the reins sure and strong. When the time came for weapons, he knew he would be ready.

The raven flocks overhead grew ever thicker. Soon it was as if great storm clouds were sailing across the face of the sun, turning the usually clear day that followed a snowstorm into gloom. Several times a gang of ravens dived upon him, as if impatient for him and his horse to die. They would fly at his horse's nose, causing it to shy and rear, and mockingly buzz the eagle they hated on his saddlebow.

But Orhan carried Zunjebei without hood or leash, and when the great raptor's patience finally gave, it launched itself into the ravens in an explosion of black feathers. Crimson droplets rained then froze onto Orhan's beard, and his horse crushed broken black things beneath its hooves.

Zunjebei returned to his saddle perch, and the remaining ravens flapped back skyward, still mocking.

And Orhan reined back, hard, for the parting curtain of ravens had revealed a fateful sight. A mere mile away, his quarry had been brought to bay by the gathered wolf packs, and had formed a circle on a low rise where they fought a last grim battle against hundreds of the carnivores. There were only some forty men left, all dismounted now, fighting only with swords and glaives, for it seemed their arrows were exhausted. But several miles beyond them rose a taller hill, and that hill was crowned by an ominous mass of stone over which floated the crimson and gold banners of the Wulong Empire. An imperial border outpost!

Several balls of flame shot into the air from the circle of raiders. It was a signal. Dimly above the baying of the attacking wolves Orhan heard the clangor of a great bronze gong in answer, and he knew that in minutes the fortress' gates would open to vomit forth squadrons of armored cavalry. He marked the tall figure in gold-shot emerald green robes instead of armor as the man threw something amid the ravening wolves, upon which there was a loud explosion throwing a dozen or more broken wolf bodies into the air.

Orhan eyed the black horsetails of the banner stolen from Toktengri's tomb as they danced in the wind, at the very center of the raiders' circle. To recover it, he would have to cut his way through what looked like all the wolves between Tashkarghan and Tali, the west and east ends of the steppe, through the surviving Wulongan raiders, face a sorcerer, then likely have to cut his way back out through the fort's cavalry.

Orhan Timur laughed out loud. The way the gods were dealing with him, he was surprised they hadn't thrown in a hundred Lakhmaristani war elephants and a few dragons for him to face as well. But even if they had, he still had everything to gain, and nothing more to lose.

"Well, brother Zunjebei, here we are. I'm riding that way," he addressed the eagle as he took it onto his arm. "If you would live, I suggest you go now." The eagle only spread its wings and gave him a proud stare. "No? You sure? Then come! What is life, against the chance to win all under heaven, eh? Fly with me!"

He threw Zunjebei into the air. Then he produced the vial of restorative and made the horse drink the last few drops he had reserved for this moment. After it had swallowed all the liquid the horse gave an earsplitting neigh

of renewed fire, and at that Orhan spurred it into the last gallop.

With the eagle as his spearhead, he tore into the ring of wolves. With his great talons Zunjebei would rake at the wolves turning to attack Orhan and his horse, then wheel and zoom away, only to return from another direction as he had been trained. That thinned away the wolves attacking him, allowing Orhan to cut down those that got past the eagle without slowing down. A glance behind his shoulder though showed the gray and black mass reforming behind him. He wondered if the wolves would stop attacking him once he got the banner.

He dared not waste any arrows on them, though. There were only twelve left in his quiver, and those he reserved for the sorcerer and his armored soldiers.

But the bulk of the howling horde had eyes only for the ring of Wulongans, ignoring the vulnerable lone rider in their midst. *They know who desecrated Toktengri's tomb*, Orhan thought, and he gave a wolfish grin of his own, of equal savagery.

Up ahead, however, he began to hear the drumming of heavy hooves, still soft and dim with distance, growing steadily louder. He lashed his foaming steed, sorry to have to do it to one who'd served so nobly this far, but desperate now for every ounce of speed he could get. He heard yells of surprise and alarm from the Wulongans in the ring, and was surprised to find himself almost among them already.

Zunjebei screamed above him, and from the corner of his eye he saw the eagle disappearing in the direction of the mountains. Whatever gods had sent it must have told the eagle its work was done. He nocked an arrow, drew, and loosed, again and again like an automaton. Wulongan soldiers fell, choking on the shafts hammered at short range into their exposed faces or throats, swords dropping from suddenly nerveless hands. He shot his last arrow at point blank range, between the eyes of a screaming maniac who left the formation to spit the horse through with a glaive.

Then he crashed into the ring of men.

There was yet another explosion and an acrid stench behind him, and he heard Lao Cheng cursing. The sorcerer had missed. A helmetless Wulongan soldier sidestepped the horse and tried to saber him from his left, seeing Orhan had no shield, but Orhan smote down, his scimitar crunching through the skull. Glaives thrust and hewed at his prancing steed, which danced aside from some of the blades while Orhan parried the others.

All the throttled fury of the past few days was burning in his veins now as he found release in battle. He had been betrayed, his homeland invaded, his tribe's most sacred site desecrated — and an empire-granting treasure was almost in his grasp. With a hoarse snarl he spurred forward again, ducked beneath a thrusting polearm, opened a Wulongan's throat with a flick of the scimitar's tip, shifted cat-like in the saddle to knock away a glaive chopping down from his other side, and then he was at the banner of black horsetails.

As he reached his left hand to take it, a green-robed form leaped before him, a saber in one hand and casting a powder that blossomed into a noxious green cloud at him. Lao Cheng! The horse breathed it in, screamed, and collapsed, its mouth and nose oozing blood and slime. But Orhan Timur was no longer there. Wary as a leopard, he'd slipped out of the saddle even as the cloud would have reached his face, and he'd closed his eyes and held his breath.

Even then, Orhan felt his face

burning. He hit the ground rolling, instinctively changing direction just in time. Lao Cheng's blade bit into the earth mere inches from his head. He lashed out with a foot, trying to kick the sorcerer's legs from beneath him, but Lao Cheng leaped over the kick, then came down with another whistling cut that Orhan barely rolled away from. He continued rolling, saw a Wulongan soldier lifting a glaive over his head, and bounced to his knees to sink his scimitar into the soldier's groin, beneath the armor's skirts.

Then Lao Cheng was upon him again, and Orhan was reeling back as he parried one cunning strike after another. The Wulongan's saber would dart toward Orhan's face, then suddenly twist to sweep at his legs, begin to slash at his neck then swerve to bite at his sword arm, never the same target twice, stretching all the nomad chieftain's skill and speed to turn them in time. Their curved blades were silvery blurs that ground sparks from each other every time they met, every block sending bone-shaking shocks of force that threatened even Orhan's iron grip on his sword.

Eunuch his opponent may have been, but Lao Cheng was unmistakably a born swordsman and honed by true masters, and Orhan suspected his strength had been sorcerously enhanced. For every trick he tried, Lao Cheng had the perfect counter – and as his own breath grew ragged, he realized with alarm that the invigorating potion was starting to wear off.

The pounding of hooves beyond was now loud as kettle-drums.

Desperate with the new threat approaching, Orhan faked a strike at the shoulder then swept in low with a powerful cut to the stomach. Lao Cheng saw through the feint, laughed as he deflected Orhan's scimitar away,

then sent his point flying toward Orhan's unarmored breast. The saber tore a burning red line across his ribs as Orhan desperately twisted aside. That however allowed Lao Cheng to knock the scimitar from his hand. Then Lao Cheng's following kick crashed into his abdomen, folding Orhan over.

The eunuch began to say something contemptuous in Wulongan as he raised his sword for the decapitating stroke.

His senses still reeling, Orhan failed to understand a word from Lao Cheng despite his fluency in Wulongan. But he could not miss the way the eunuch suddenly went from gloating to a shocked grunt of pain, and the deposed khan raised his eyes to see Lao Cheng reeling in surprise, a Wulongan arrow in the back of his thigh.

"Surrender, Lao Cheng! By order of Prince Sun Jian, Lord Governor of Tali, you are to be taken prisoner and interrogated for your crimes and conspiracies against our august master! Reveal your secrets and accomplices, and the Prince may yet spare your miserable life, or at least grant you a quick death. Will you surrender?" demanded the Wulongan officer leading the cavalry.

Lao Cheng glared at the officer, his features gone from coolly contemptuous to bestial wrath. "Sun Jian! When word of my death by his order reaches the capital, Hou Yao, your exiled prince and all his cronies will be doomed! If the Emperor fails to see you executed by the Death of a Thousand Cuts, my brethren in the secret order I belong to will give you an end infinitely more slow and painful!"

"My life is a low price to see a poisonous scorpion removed from my prince's path," Hou Yao said easily. "Besides, who will bear the tale back to the capital? Your men are already all dead." He gestured, and Lao Cheng flicked his eyes left and right, Orhan marking the dangerous glint in them as Hou Yao's men divided into two teams, the larger one holding off the wolves, while another squad shot or speared Lao Cheng's few remaining soldiers.

Orhan thought he saw the eunuch palming something from his robe's wide sleeve. "You give me no choice, Hou Yao," Lao Cheng yelled. "I'll escape yet, and with my treasure!"

Suddenly the eunuch flung something to the ground, and there was a small explosion of eldritch green flames and smoke that fully enveloped him. Horses screamed and reared at the stench. Then men and horses screamed again, even louder, at what came forth from that unnatural cloud.

Instead of the eunuch's slim form, what leaped out from the viridian smoke was a monstrous creature at least nine feet tall, warty green skin pebbled with protruding nodules of bone, an ox-like head crowned with mighty black horns, a long lizard's tail, and legs that ended in black hooves. Its face, however, was unmistakably Lao Cheng's.

Running with impossible lightness on its hooves, the creature seized the horsetail banner in one hand, then hit Hou Yao's horse with a great fist that knocked the steed over, pinning its hapless rider beneath it. The cavalrymen beside Hou Yao tried to charge the creature with their glaives, but it contemptuously knocked the heavy polearms aside, then its fist came down on one horseman's head to burst the helmet and skull beneath into red ruin. The other horseman's mount threw him in its panic, and then the creature was through them and running for the mountains with Toktengri's banner.

The banner!

Orhan Timur was galvanized back into action. He scooped up his dropped scimitar, grabbed the reins of the brained cavalryman's horse, and leaped into its saddle. Then he was spurring after Lao Cheng, or what had been Lao Cheng, before any of the terrified Wulongan cavalrymen could follow.

As Orhan Timur closed in on the creature it turned, swinging a great fist. Orhan ducked beneath it, then slashed at the arm.

The sword bounced off.

He blasphemed in consternation, wheeled the horse around, and attacked the creature again. What had been Lao Cheng blocked Orhan's powerful cut with an arm, then laughed in terrifying glee as once more the keen edge failed to bite.

"Ha, no steel can cut me! I did not expect my potion to work so well! Ha, how does it feel to fight an invulnerable foe, little man?" Lao Cheng mocked.

"If you were truly invulnerable, you wouldn't be running away," Orhan taunted back. "Or is it true eunuchs lose all courage when they're cut?"

Lao Cheng howled and charged the horseman. Orhan wheeled the horse away, glad it was a trained cavalry mount that obeyed him despite its fear, and Lao Cheng's enlarged fist pitted the earth where they'd been. Orhan found a case of javelins hanging from the saddlebow and pitched one at Lao Cheng's head, aiming for the eye. It struck the ox head in the cheek instead, but again the steel refused to bite.

Lao Cheng roared in frustration and charged again.

Again, Orhan darted away. A hazy plan was in the nomad chief's cat-agile mind. Even as he'd launched into pursuit, he was already speculating on the limits to Lao Cheng's invulnerability. There had to be limits. Else why would the monster have fled? *Perhaps by maddening the monster further and wearing it down I can trick it into revealing its weakness*, Orhan thought. *Sometimes sheer persistence can be the highest form of cunning.*

But even as he spat yet another gibe, Orhan saw Lao Cheng suddenly pause and give him an unmistakably frightened stare. Then the creature wheeled about and ran again for the mountains, and this time Orhan's horse was hard-pressed to catch up with it. Orhan leaned low over the saddle and yelled into the horse's ear to make it run harder. Were his eyes tricking him, or had the monster shrunk a little? Was it still shrinking even as he pounded closer?

Suddenly they were past the creature, and Orhan whirled in the saddle. Had the giant stumbled? No. It was no longer there. Instead, the naked form of Lao Cheng was gasping on all fours, the banner forgotten beneath him. Now Orhan understood what the monster's weakness had been. Like the potion that had revitalized him and his horse, its effect wore off with time – perhaps the more drastic the effect, the faster it wore off?

Orhan rode slowly up to the eunuch. "Leave me the banner of Toktengri, and you may go," he said, with the Murjen respect for a good opponent.

Lao Cheng struggled to his feet, mouth working, his face a terrible mask of hate. Believing the eunuch was casting some spell against him, Orhan rose in his stirrups and dealt Lao Cheng a mighty slash that sent the head and part of a shoulder flying from the man's trunk.

He dismounted and picked up the banner. But even as Orhan resumed the saddle, the cavalry captain Hou Yao and his squadron came pounding up, and the nomad raised his sword for the last fight.

"You will not have the sacred banner of Toktengri while I live. And if you want those hordes of wolves and ravens to disperse instead of ravaging your border villages, you will let me go," Orhan warned.

But Hou Yao bowed from the saddle, causing Orhan to raise an eyebrow in surprise.

"You are free to go wherever you wish, my Lord Orhan Timur, and take the banner with you," Hou Yao said, speaking in fluent Western Murjen, which few of the soldiers understood. Orhan immediately saw he meant their conversation to go uncomprehended.

"We have met?"

"I was honored to be part of your escort when you came to negotiate the last peace treaty, Lord Orhan," the Wulongan officer smiled. "It took me a bit, but eventually I recalled who you were. I would advise you to be far from the border soon, my lord, for a messenger from Jungar Khan rode to Tali with a letter for the Governor, and rumors have been flying back of an, ah, unfortunate incident on the steppes. It's also being said that in the letter, Jungar Khan promised a hundred thousand taels in gold to anyone who'd bring you or your head back to him."

"I am surprised you're not tempted," Orhan observed wryly.

"I am. But in taking on the demon that Lao Cheng became, you saved many of my men, and I owe you thanks for that. And there is the matter of that banner." Hou Yao nodded at the black horsetail standard in Orhan's left hand. Like other khan's war banners, it was made of horse tails hung from an ornately incised metal drum with a domed top. Unlike Orhan's similar standard, however, which the Wulongan border troops had seen all too often, this one was topped not with a spear-like finial but with a gold-plated skull that Hou Yao would have called human, save that it had long fangs.

"We had heard a Khereyid tribesman had come to Tali spouting rumors about Tokten-

gri's tomb, and when Lao Cheng, who had long been suspected of studying the dark arts, disappeared with him our prince guessed what he was after. Lao Cheng must have planned to present it to the Emperor, or use it in some dark ritual, but either way it would have been used to harm Prince Sun Jian," Hou Yao continued. "But I see the legendary curse on it is true. The banner should go back where it belongs."

Orhan regarded the banner, then looked at the wolves that had gathered a mere hundred yards behind the horsemen. The gray terrors of the steppe were now all sitting attentively, red tongues lolling as if in mocking laughter, their slanted eyes fixed upon himself.

"I had thought to keep it because it always brought victory, but I, too, see now it would be better to return it," Orhan said slowly. It was hard to give up on his original intention, but after what he had seen he now saw that would be a mistake. He would have to find other weapons against Jungar.

"For what it's worth, my lord, I heartily agree."

Orhan kneed his horse into a walk. "You can do me another service, Captain Hou Yao. Whisper a word in Prince Sun Jian's ear when you can. Tell him, as one exiled prince to another, that if ever he thinks of a way we can benefit each other to regain our proper places, I will be listening."

"I will do that, my lord," said Hou Yao, and bowed.

The weather had turned again, with the fickleness of weather close by the shadow of great mountains. Racing gray clouds had again shrouded the sky, and snow was starting to fall in thick, billowing blankets. Like a ghost out of legend himself, Orhan Timur disappeared into the swirling white pall, the skull-topped horsetail banner fading

into the gloom like a departing angel of death.

But under his breath the nomad chief muttered, for the wolves were scattering away from him back to their old hunting ranges on the steppe, and they would be driving all the game away.

And he was still hungry.

ABOUT THE AUTHOR

Dariel R. A. Quiogue is a writer-photographer from the Philippines. In 1977, he was simultaneously exposed to Star Wars, Herodotus, Homer, Edgar Rice Burroughs, and Robert E. Howard, and his brain has never been the same since. He now writes fantasy and science fiction in his spare time, flavored by his fascination for history, science, the sea, and the richness and diversity of Asian cultures. His creative motto is "Simple stories, powerfully told." Quiogue's works have appeared in *The Best of Heroic Fantasy Quarterly Volume I*, the *Philippine Speculative Fiction Annual Volume 7*, *Rakehell*, and his self-published story collection *Swords of the Four Winds*.

www.amazon.com/-/e/ B00GXRIMFY

swashbucklingplanets .wordpress.com

The Ember Inside

by Remco van Straten & Angeline B. Adams

Blood footed, strong-tooth, bear-skinned Bärsk remembers:
Witch-bred, bear fed, in his lair contented;
When men came, bearing flame, Bärsk soon lamented,
When horse borne highborn, slayed his kin for game.
Then fate turned, with hatred burning, he defied surrender,
His axe swept, and gore-flecked Bärsk became their bane.

- The Lay of Bärsk the Bloodied

Kaila's eyes narrowed behind the edge of her sword. Already short, she stood crouched, her head low. Yet, with feet planted wide and muscles straining the fabric of her short-sleeved tunic, everything in her spoke of strength.

"By the fur of my mother, which I wear as my witness," she growled.

Sebastien stood behind her, tall and slight in contrast. He clutched Ymke's walking stick as a makeshift sword. He squinted, and his voice was a low whisper: "I'll hunt down all who wronged me, cut their heads from their ruined bodies."

"And laugh as their corpses hang from the highest trees," Kaila roared. Her sword arm shot up, her blade's tip glancing off the low beams of the cabin's ceiling. Ymke gave them a slow handclap from the makeshift bed in front of the fireplace where she'd made herself as comfortable as she could.

"Thank you, thank you. I think I've heard enough about Berk the Brutal. The neighbours have already given us the evil eye, and we can do without the shouting and you trashing the place."

"Ah now, Ymke," Kaila said. She slid her sword back into its scabbard and flung herself down beside her. "Don't tell me it doesn't get your blood rushing," she said, her face close to her lover's.

Ymke rolled her eyes. "I think not; it's altogether too rich for me. It's more something for a growing lad like Sebastien, surely."

"Hey, that's unfair," Sebastien said, and in replacing Ymke's walking stick, stumbled over the previous night's sack of loot.

"Careful, boy!" said Kaila. "We still have to fence that."

Sebastien recovered himself. "As I was saying, Bärsk is very popular with all manner of people."

"Such as you'll find in beer halls and public squares," said Ymke.

"Anyway," Kaila interjected. "Your letter?"

Ymke unfolded the letter that had caused all the excitement.

"*To the lady Ymke,*" she began.

"Haven't we come up in the world!" Sebastien exclaimed. "Our Ymke's a lady now!"

"Well, each of us has our part to play, and this is one I have to work very hard at with you two fiends reminding me of my humble origins," Ymke replied, yet the arm she had around Kaila tempered her words. In turn, Kaila's hard, calloused hand kneaded the muscle of her bad hip. It felt good. Ymke cleared her throat and started anew.

"*To the lady Ymke,*

I most humbly desire you to pardon my boldness. I have friends among our local parchment makers, and they bring me tales of one who gives them her custom, who has shown them her works, by which they have been most heartily impressed.

You in turn may have chanced upon my own literary endeavours. Alack, in the pursuance of my craft, I overreached myself and, in so doing, was betrayed by my eyesight. That being the case, for the past year it has been sadly necessary for me to take a rest cure, hence my sojourn here.

If I may be so direct: I find that I miss literary company, and I therefore beg that you might indulge an old man by partaking with him of tea, in two days' time, at the hour of three.

Your servant,
Sigismond of Santhen, known for The Lay of Bärsk, The Horn of King Arthorius, Crimson Trail, &c."

"That's amazing." Sebastien jumped up. "Tell me you're going."

"I think not," said Ymke, folding the letter back up. "He probably thinks he can have me work for him in exchange for flattery. I don't need that."

"Please, dear! You *must* call me Sigi."

"Well, then, Sigi. I gather from your letter that you have read my work?"

Seated in the verse-maker's cluttered parlour, Ymke was not altogether happy with the way he looked at her. Perhaps, she thought, she should have let Kaila and Sebastien come with her after all.

"Ymke of the Barren North," Sigismond started. He held up his hands, his spread fingers touching the imaginary letters of her name in the space between them. "A bright, talented young thing who seems of late to have abandoned the arts. Whereto has this talent been frittered, I wonder."

He extended the pause almost palpably, as if offering Ymke his hand, to aid her in delicately stepping across a filthy street.

"I've not done so badly, for an itinerant scribe, and I assure you that there has been no—to borrow your term—frittering," she said. Then, after a pause she let drag uncomfortably: "We're a direct people, the Cruonhingans. The 'Barren North' leaves nowhere to hide. I'm familiar with your work, and don't see why someone writing such crude narratives would seek out the likes of me. I sense that you didn't invite me here only for tea, so tell me what it is you want."

He surrendered himself to his chair. "Ymke, I will meet your candour with my own. The well has run dry. The rest cure for my eyes, to which I alluded in my missive, is in fact an exile. My circumstances..." here he tailed off, and his eyes roamed around a room dim even on that glorious summer afternoon, "...are reduced. You disparage my work in my own home, such as it is, and yet I cannot deny: the gavel you wield is held by many. You had best hear now what it is to fall out of favour, for it comes to every scribe at one time or another."

Ymke noticed the accent of the cultivated Santhener giving way here and there to a more rural lilt.

"I've travelled the length and breadth of this country, and was welcomed by merchants, noblemen, and princes whose largesse paid me richly for stories of bloodlust and conquest—a world of the imagination, beyond their dusty halls and tedious responsibilities, for our betters seek the carnal, visceral thrill of the baser pleasures. And by the gods, did I give it to them!"

His hands now clutched his thighs and Ymke saw, despite his heavy robes, how thin they were.

"And then?" she prompted. It elicited a glimmer of satisfaction.

"And then," he sighed, "suddenly it would no longer do. My patrons' children, first in enraptured silence at the fireside, grew up, and as youth must, they had their own ideas about the world. 'Is this what's best in life?' one duke's daughter asked one evening. 'Murder and violence, boots sliding over innards? What is the value in all of this? Where is the humanity?' I gestured at the window. 'Out there,' I said, and I confess I was intemperate. 'There's your humanity, if only you'd care to look.' And I shouldn't have done that."

"Let me guess: they reminded you that despite rubbing shoulders with them, you still were not one of them?"

"Invitations I had been able to count on for years failed to materialise, and what custom I got was devoid of the pleasantries I'd come to expect. Eventually, I was cast away altogether, like a bone stripped clean of meat."

"I've met more kinds of people than most," Ymke said slowly. "And you're not the first person to share a story filled with sorrow. Tea doesn't come cheap, so I ask you again: what is it you hope to buy with it?"

"And there shall be tea, absolutely. What I want, Ymke, is *your* story. They want humanity? I shall give them the true story of a girl who survived the war-torn wasteland of Cruonhinga and somehow made it in the world outside. A brave cripple—they'll love it. You of all people must know this. People love to compare themselves to the less fortunate, to believe they would offer succour, sanctuary, to such a person if given the chance."

Ymke stood and drew her cloak about her. "Are you mad? That's not my story and never was. I'll not have my life reduced to a tale of pity or admonishment, and frankly, you overestimate the public appetite for stories of cripples. We're less than welcome *in real life.*"

He raised his eyes to meet hers, and it was them, and not the hands he held up in a gesture of defeat, that made her falter for a moment. Undeniably it was pain she read in them, pain and shame.

"You know what it is to be unseen," she said, more carefully. "You could be more than just an amusement to be discarded. So why conjure another's life into a simplistic morality tale?"

Sigismond rose too. "Dear lady, desperation erodes my manners. I crave your pardon—think it over, at least, while you have that bowl of tea."

She considered the man, and his faded wallpaper, his motheaten curtains, and his drab, dusty ornaments.

"Fine. One bowl," she said.

When it arrived, she accepted the bowl, politely ignoring its chipped rim. A pleasant aroma came from the russet tea leaves, intensifying as the old storyteller carefully added hot water. He saw her enjoyment of the fragrance.

"A very fine blend. I've a little man who gets it directly from the East."

They fell to slow, contempla-

tive drinking, and the old man, pretending their earlier barbed conversation hadn't happened, regaled Ymke with the provenance of various objects in the room. The heat became stifling, and her nods and polite smile were forced.

"This is something special," he said, setting down his bowl. He lifted down a sword that hung from the wall by a chain and removed it from its scabbard. "Would you believe I received this from the Duke of Arguinta?"

Its ornate hilt was gilded and inlaid with coloured glass, but the blade was cast metal, and blunt.

"No, I would not," she said, truthfully. Her own voice appeared to come from outside her.

Would Kaila find it poorly balanced? she wondered. *I should ask her.*

"Look closer," Sigismond said. He raised the sword to her face at an angle that let the dusty sunlight play upon the inlaid pattern. The light became liquid, moving sensually.

What's happening? she wanted to ask him. He withdrew the sword, but the light continued to dance before her, and she felt him take the bowl from her hands. He smiled and spoke to her. Did he require an answer? No, he was looking at her as if she'd been speaking, willing her to continue. She found the thread of what she'd been saying—apparently.

I am sixteen years old.
Ymke trudged over the frozen ground, making her way back from the well, her steps marking over and over the number of years she had lived. She fancied that the water itself threatened to freeze with every step, though it came from deeper in the earth, from a place where life still flowed, where goodness was still kept. There was little warmth in Ymke's life up here on the surface of the world, on the farm called Sunne, except for the righteous

11

ember of hate she kept in her heart for the Elminghas.

When the world threatened to choke all hope from Ymke, she remembered her father's last act on her behalf: his refusal to marry her off to Reider Elmingha, the autumn before. That had been over a year ago, and her father had died that night.

Her fate, she had eventually understood, had been circling them both since the day she was born. There truly was no soil in that part of Cruonhinga that would not one day become Elmingha's: the smallholders, so they said at market, were merely looking after their parcels of land for him.

Ymke wondered what her life would have been like if their harvest had not failed that last year. If the old man had not demanded she marry him. If her father had lived.

Reider Elmingha was dead now too, and together with farm, lands, and cattle, Ymke had been passed on to his son. Creil Elmingha had softened somewhat since his father died, but she could not find it in herself to warm to him.

Ymke thought about the ember in her heart and lugged the bucket into the scullery. The sun was hardly up, and already her hip ached.

I am eighteen years old, and my son is a year old today.

He had been a heavy, dragging, bellyful of rage; a fire that she feared would extinguish her own small light. She'd hated how the child had distorted her body and made the veins stand out on her legs. She hated how the women on the farm cooed over her, or rather the thing that grew inside her, and how they made her lie down when she cried out in pain over the unbearable weight on her leg "for the baby."

She remembered little of the night he ripped her open, except

that in the small hours, as the wet nurse fed the mewling thing, she had finally realised she was not going to die. There was a hardiness in her that, though deeply buried, was not beyond calling upon, and when her milk finally came, and she could dutifully suckle the thing that Creil Elm-

ingha had planted within her, she kept her own counsel.

It seemed to Ymke that she might have had another life—just around the corner or reflected in the surface of the milk that leaked from her. First the notion came to her in the long nights in which she couldn't sleep from the

12

pain in her leg. Then it began to encroach on the sleep-starved daze she slipped into while doing her chores. Strangely, it had the quality of a memory. She saw herself, or a girl like her, out in the world: riding a horse in a forest, moving around corners in a city she'd never been to, wearing clothes she'd never owned, with her hair blowing free. She knew that she had—this other Ymke had—companions, and she had a memory of hands on her body that were nothing like Creil's. Always, Ymke would drag her mind away from these phantoms and go on with her weaving. And so, she adorned the house, adding to the fine things that Elmingha owned. She, too, was a thing Elmingha owned.

From the littlest maid to the most crabbed old crone, the other women on Elmingha's place never took to her. She was their mistress, but also their charge—not right in the head, they thought. She observed the conversations suddenly hushed at her approach and the subtle hand gestures to ward off evil. They kept from her sharp knives, needles, and anything else she might do harm with. "It's not safe, Mistress," they'd say, "for the baby."

They smiled at her, of course, and asked her what she was thinking about. She just smiled back and let her gaze glide to the ever-present child.

Still, she squirrelled away every little bit they let slip and so learned, plant by plant, the recipes to draughts to purge her womb. No matter how Creil might use her, she would not bear him another child. The small store of plants she'd gathered always disappeared eventually, though nothing was ever said, just as she never mentioned the charms she found under the boy's pillows and hidden in his clothes. She just became more careful, and fed her dismay to the ember inside her that continued to burn.

And just as she'd closed her heart and mind to Creil, she closed her legs, and he in turn grew colder with every passing year. He gathered around him a band of young men, and she watched them practice in the yard with crudely forged swords.

"You'll thank me one day," he said to her, catching the cold look that belied the smile below it, and she imagined she would.

I am twenty-three years old. I have two sons now, despite my best efforts. My youngest is four.

Both the boys resembled her, or so people said, yet she couldn't love them any more for that. She kept them quiet by telling them stories, stretching those companions of her mind's invention over the bones of the tales from her mother's old storybook. She wondered what had happened to it: probably long gone on the pyre, along with almost everything else she'd once owned. She scrunched the thought up into a ball and fed it to her own fire, deep inside of her.

The boy who travelled with her mirror-self was skinny, with pale hair that hung around his head like a cloud. He laughed a lot, and told exaggerated tales of his kills, though he was no match for the girl who was with them. She was harder to grasp: an impression of strength and movement, more than anything.

"Her name was Kale," she told her sons. "Yes, like that cabbage you won't eat, for Kale ate every scrap, and soon she could swing the biggest sword, small though she was." She did not care if her sons ate or not, for she could not love children who stared at her all day with their father's unsettling eyes. Yet Creil cared, and as long as his heirs were healthy, he'd leave her alone. So, she persisted, urging them to eat, to sleep, to behave, while the ember inside her, nurtured all the while with her impa-

tience, hatred, and disgust, glowed as brightly as ever.

I am twenty-six, and the nearing winter makes my bones ache.

It was the first time in years that roving mercenaries brought trouble to the farm, and neither Creil nor his men were around. When a rider had come through heavy rain with word of an attack on an outlying Elmingha farm, they'd taken off, guldering and swinging their swords like children. Ymke would've shaken her head at their foolishness had she not, soon after, found herself standing at sword-point in her own kitchen. Her sons cowered behind her, clutching her skirts, and the maids lurked in the scullery in frozen terror. The war was older than anyone on the farm, but the stories of the things soldiers did to women no longer held any fear for Ymke. She knew too well what men were capable of.

The soldiers were as such men have always been. Some callow, some grey-bearded, but all bringing the surly menace of their kind.

"See my men fed, woman, and quick with it," their captain demanded. Or else, his sword added. He dripped onto the kitchen flagstones, and she took in his dishevelment. Theirs was the losing side, then. He was taller than the rest of them; blond and handsome, and he had startling blue eyes, yet was nothing like the boy in her fantasies.

A throaty laugh came from deep within her.

"So, you're in charge then," she said. "Food's in the pantry. Eat quickly, for this is Creil Elmingha's place, and when he comes back, which won't be too long, he'll not come alone."

"Perhaps there's something else we want," piped up one of the younger soldiers, a boy with bloody knuckles and a voice that still cracked a little.

"Elmingha's place, eh?" his commander said. Ymke caught the slight frown before he masked it with a sideways grin. He grabbed her chin with his free hand and forced open her mouth with his fingers. Ymke heard a gasp from one of the maids.

"She does have most of her teeth," he said, his glance then moving down and resting on the walking stick she still held. He released her and shook his head.

"Stringy peasant with a gammy leg. Worn out before her time with whelping. The rest of them aren't much better. Leave them."

She bore the insult as she bore all insults. It was not yet the time for her to burn. The rain drummed harder on the roof above.

He called out to his men to help themselves, which they did. Some slung their arms around the maids, whispered in their ears and laughed. Others tossed loaves onto the table, unhung a ham and hacked a great round cheese into pieces, then jostled for a place round the table with a scraping of chair legs and a clattering of dropped weapons. The captain ordered the boy soldier from a chair and sat down, grabbed one of the maids by the wrist, and jerked her onto his lap. Ymke ignored her anxious glances and slowly moved towards the door, the knuckles of her hand white on her walking stick, and opened it with her other hand. Her sons still clung to her. Through the rain, a cow lowed.

"You're not thinking of leaving us, are you?" the captain said. His sword, a thin blade, flicked out and stood in the doorpost before her eyes. The maid slid off his lap, and he rose, his hand still on the hilt of his blade.

"Do you think you I could outrun you if I did?" She snorted.

He winked at her, pulled his sword free and went on one knee,
smiling at her boys.

"And how about you, are you going to make a run for it?"

Her youngest nodded and her oldest stared at the man, his mouth a thin, straight line. "I am an Elmingha," he said, with all the solemnity of a nine-year-old.

The captain rose and laughed. Then his face changed abruptly. He jerked the door wider.

"Out." When the boys didn't move into the rain quickly enough, he shoved them. He looked at Ymke as he kicked the door shut, shook his head, and sat down again, turning his back to her. At the other end of the table, one of the maids shrieked and wrestled herself free from the embrace of one of the soldiers. The soldier was short and stocky, even for a southerner. Ymke's eye was first drawn to the padded jerkin, sewn with strange medallions and flecked with battlefield gore, then to a cruel sneer, and a face hidden by long, black hair. A woman, Ymke realised, though as hardy as her comrades. The soldier brushed her rain-soaked locks away and met Ymke's stare with eyes full of the contempt of a free woman for one in bondage. They were large and black-rimmed, and Ymke's breath faltered; they belonged to the girl from her dreams, though there, in the other Ymke's life, they had spoken to her with love. The ember, kept safe in her heart for all those years, flared into life, quickening her in a way that she could not allow to be seen. She wrenched her gaze away from the mercenary's, back to the door. It hadn't fully closed, and she sucked in the wet air, while the other woman worked at a hunk of bread with her dagger.

Then, above the jeers of the soldiers, and the clatter of knives and crockery, she heard hoofbeats and voices. Ymke flattened herself against the wall and waited.
The door burst open and with a gust of wind and rain Creil and his men pushed inside. The soldiers scrambled, grasping their daggers, their swords, as the men fell upon them. The table upturned, and chairs clattered backwards.

The fight was as brutal as it was short. Though Creil's men surprised and outnumbered the mercenaries, they couldn't immediately press their advantage in the cramped space. Creil and the mercenary's captain both shouted their orders, but the kitchen became a chaos of snapping bones, spurting blood, and the hoarse shouts of dying throats.

A young farmhand, whose name she couldn't remember, crashed into the wall beside Ymke, and she watched as his jaw worked up and down, and his life blood escaped though his slit throat. She turned. With a flash of red, the female soldier fell backwards at her feet. Ymke raised her stick, and as black eyes glared and teeth bared, she jammed it down beside her face. Ymke nudged sideways towards the door, and the woman scrambled through it.

Ymke followed her outside, just a few difficult steps on the waterlogged ground. The woman grabbed one of Creil's horses by the bridle and heaved herself onto it.

"Kale!" Ymke called to her, and she turned round and frowned, but then she slapped the horse's flank and galloped off. The wind dropped in her wake, and the rain drizzled and then ceased.

Creil and his men were victorious, and they emerged shortly afterwards. A fair few of them had died, or would never work the farm again, yet that did not stop them from shouting their elation, bragging, and slapping each other's backs. A few of the soldiers were bundled out amongst them: some youths, who were used for sport in the farm-yard before they were finally killed, and their captain, who had the honour of being hung from the farm's ancient oak.

"A shame in a way, good look-ing devil like him," one maid called out, as the rope snapped taut.

"And doesn't he dance hand-somely," answered another, tit-tering.

Slowly, his limbs stopped jerking, and his body finally hung still. He was facing Ymke.

"He's still got eyes for the mistress, even now!" the maid screeched and laughed. Then, noticing the sudden silence, her hand flew to her mouth.

Ymke managed to find her sons and trailed them back inside, where her husband waited for her. Creil was furious: furious to have found the farm they'd rid-den off to deserted and then, rid-ing back with that particular thirst unslaked, to find his own home defiled. He was furious with his men, whom he'd drilled with pride, but who had made a complete hash of the fight when it came to it. Most of all, he was furious with his wife.

"What did he do to you? Did he take you?" he demanded of her.

"He did not take me. He left me unharmed, as you can see."

He slammed his fist into the doorpost, and Ymke couldn't tell whether he was angry because he thought she might be lying, or be-cause the soldiers hadn't wanted her, his property.

My eldest son is ten years old to-*day. I am twenty-seven years old. But from now on I will stop count-ing my age.*

The harvest feast had come, and her eldest boy was at the cen-tre of it. Though his looks still favoured hers, when she led him out to the field, he walked with the long, measured pace of his fa-ther. Though the harvest was a task that absorbed everyone on the farm, and everyone from farmer to farmhand was welcome as the barn doors were put on trestles in the farmyard and laden with food, this part was for the family alone. It was time to cut the last sheaf, always the task of the eldest child. Done right, it would bring good luck for the next year.

"Not so fast," Ymke called out, as she followed him over the stubble with difficulty.

Her childhood farm stood on the horizon, a ruin now and a home only to pigeons. The sun hung low in the sky above it, an ugly orange ball. Soon it would set and when the evening shad-ows brought the chill, everyone would flock to the bonfire the men had built. They would ex-pect Creil to light the fire as their lord and provider. She had best hurry, she thought, and reached for the fire inside her; let it fill her unwilling legs, her heaving lungs, and pounding heart.

How pitifully small had been the fire Ymke's father had lit, that evening before Creil's father had come for her. Yet, they'd enjoyed its warmth and blessing, even as the fire of the farm Sunne winked on the horizon.

Creil was already standing far into the field, a large scarecrow of a man holding the scythe, and his son couldn't wait to be with him. He was an unloving father, yet where she saw coldness, his boy saw strength. His absence had made him an almost mythical being to both children, while she—well.

Her husband swayed a little, though there was no wind. There had been plenty of good ale at the celebration. She'd made sure of that.

"Did you bring a blindfold?" Creil's face was a shadow.

She had, and she tied it round their boy's eyes. It was a simple handkerchief: large and red, with white flowers embroidered on its corners. She remembered her fa-ther standing behind her, that last time, as he blindfolded her with the same handkerchief. When the Elminghas' black carriage had come for her, she'd still had it in the pocket of her dress.

Her husband handed his son the scythe, letting the boy grope for it. Then he stood back, his jaw clenched, and watched as his son awkwardly moved the blade be-fore him.

"Come on son, what are you; an old maid with a broom? More to the left," he said, and, with a sigh: "Your other left."

The boy stopped and tore off the blindfold. Except for the tears that glinted in his eyes, his face mirrored his father's.

Ymke's flame leapt. *Now*, it said. The voice was her own, and at the same time not hers.

She discarded her stick and stepped forward. She ignored the pain searing through her leg, pic-tured it as a lightning rod come from the soil to feed her flame.

"Give me that," she said. "I'll show you how it's done."

Her son watched as she moved the scythe back, her hands tight on the grips, and she felt the boy's eyes still on her as she turned, the fire coursing through her. A memory of her younger self flashed through her; the feel-ing of the blade cutting the last sheaf. The blade she held now met Creil's leg, severing his foot above the ankle. He wasn't screaming yet when he fell to his knees, and he would no more, for her second stroke caught his neck.

She looked from the father, spread out in the stubble, to the son. She would not take him with her, nor his brother, but would go alone to find the place where her fire could burn full and true at last.

"You're the lord of Sunne now, Reider Elmingha," she told the boy. "Do with it what you will."

Then she strode off, leaning on the scythe.

In her waning years, Ymke would once again feel the pull of an impossible memory. It seemed that she had been invited somewhere, that a strange man peered at her. It seemed that he wanted something from her.

Around her bed stood those who loved her. She felt her breath flee and the life retreat from her limbs. *At least it's an end to the pain.*

She closed her eyes and smiled. *And let them wonder what I'm thinking about.*

Then she waited.

"Ymke?"

Oh, for the gods' sake. I'm dying here, and still, they need me?

"Ymke." A hand on her shoulder shook her gently.

Go away!

"Go away," she whispered.

"Ymke, wake up!" More urgent now. She recognised that voice. Fancy that; the girl she imagined during her time on the farm. She hadn't thought about her for years.

How—?

She opened her eyes with difficulty.

What was her name again?

"Kale?"

As Ymke woke up slowly, the long life she'd led slipped away like sand between spread fingers. Her mind would stand no emptiness, however, and while that life dissolved, memories of her life with Kaila and Sebastien took its

16

place; a life in which her father had lived past that harvest night, and though they'd left their farm, she'd never been a bride of the Elminghas.

Kaila held her hands and gazed at her, eyes full of love and concern. Sigismond of Santhen sat opposite her as before, though somewhat roughed up, and the door behind him hung forlornly in a splintered frame. Around his feet lay a scattering of vellum and the wreck of a small portable writing desk. A large ink stain on the carpet between them reminded her of Creil's blood in the cornfield.

"My memories... that was not my past," she shook the image from her mind and stared at the old man. "None of it happened like that! What did you give me?"

"It's more a matter of what you gave me," Sigismond replied. He gestured at the papers, which Ymke saw, even in the dimness of the room, were filled with a feverish scribble.

"Alack, I cannot use any of it. You have no talent for tragedy, Ymke! I wanted meekness, a story to make others weep. You disapprove of my Bärsk, and yet you gave me such hatred and bloodshed!"

His hurt indignation offended her even more than that he'd drugged her. She reached for her walking stick, but her fingers, slower to recover than her mind, fumbled, and it fell. Her knees buckled when she tried to stand without it.

"Sit down, love," Kaila said, easing her back into the chair. "He's going nowhere, and we've got time."

Ymke leaned her head against Kaila's chest and closed her eyes, if only for a moment, lest that other life reclaim her.

"That's right," she said, "we've got all the time."

They walked home along the river, the city's life around them shifting as the daytime workers went home, and the night birds began to emerge. While most of the lifetime Ymke's mind had conjured had disappeared, odd notions remained, like the feeling that she'd eaten nothing but the food of the north for many years. Kaila wasn't a good cook, far from it, yet she knew how to add flavour to otherwise bland fodder, and Ymke's mouth watered at the thought of their supper.

"I can't believe you took that ugly thing," she said, nudging at the sword that hung at Kaila's hip, opposite her customary blade.

"It may be ugly, and useless as a sword, but the gems on it are real. They'll keep us in rent for a while, once I've pried them from the metal. And you certainly took your time reading Sigismond's notes on his previous victims," said Kaila. "What did you find?"

"That I wasn't as unique as he had me believe, nor he as lonely. The notes were sketchy, and he'd have a hard time spinning good yarns from them. But his journal! He scribbled away in it, all the dirty little secrets that didn't fit with what he wanted to believe of those great, wealthy houses. Had he made clever use of them, he might live far better than he does now."

"Then why didn't he? I prefer good old-fashioned gold, but Sebastien was right—information is currency too."

"Same reason he didn't sell the gems off the sword—perverse loyalty to his old patrons. It's a sad thing to rely on others to tell you who you are."

Kaila laughed. "I guess Sigismond will get his story after all: He'll be dreaming for a while yet on all that tea I made him drink."

They had reached the top of their street, and Kaila slowed her pace, and frowned.

"Still, you only went today because I pressed you, and I put you in danger," she said. "You shouldn't have had to go out for someone to appreciate your work. Will you read me something tonight?"

"Oh, Kaila. You were there for me when it counted. You always are. You know, quite a few poems are about you. And maybe you can tell me more about Bärsk. It seems I have more of a taste for bloodshed than I thought. But first, what do you say we send Sebastien on another errand, and write another chapter in our story together?"

She turned to Kaila. "You know, I missed you an awful lot."

ABOUT THE AUTHORS

The work of Angeline B. Adams (she/her) and Remco van Straten (he/him) is steeped in a shared love for folklore and history, and is firmly rooted in Angeline's Northern Irish childhood and the northern Dutch coast where Remco grew up.

Their fiction has appeared in various anthologies, and their collection *The Red Man and Others* was nominated for a Robert E. Howard Foundation Award, alongside Angeline's talk on disability and the roots of Heroic Fantasy.

turniplanterns.wordpress.com/ newsletter

Old Moon Over Irukad
by David C. Smith

She was most attractive, the young woman watching Virissa from across the noisy crowded public room. Beautiful eyes, perfect cheek bones, and red hair, which the fighter preferred.

They watched each other as the coarse patrons of this hole moved back and forth between them. What was she doing here, offering herself as bait? On an adventure, surely. And the unsmiling titan standing beside her, no doubt here for her protection. Probably with her family for years, this guardian. Wealthy family, certainly, with a daughter who had never been tamed by them. And this powerful man, all chest and arms and scarred face, capable of managing any of the hearties here tonight.

Virissa kept her eyes on her.

Beautiful young woman.

Seduce her?

Or take the bauble that rested at her throat, a gem surely worth a small fortune?

"...heard a single word I've said."

Virissa reluctantly turned to face Edrion, seated opposite her.

"Have you?"

"I have not," she confessed.

Edrion looked at the beauty across the public room and admitted, "Surely a prize. But not tonight."

Virissa frowned. "He's here?"

Edrion nodded toward the open door of this place, where certain kinds of men and women loitered and a tall man wholly in various shades of gray, robe and boots and beard and all, stood awaiting them. Knives in his belt, too. And no rings or baubles visible. He was about his business and nothing else.

He stood beneath old carvings set in a mantel above the wide entry to the tavern, painted busts done in oak hundreds of years old of the nine founders of Irukad. Most visitors to the tavern avoided looking at the carvings. Each was distinguished by some mark or sign, as was common with the old tribal people then. One had a formidable nose and protruding jaw. Another had a streak of white hair interrupting the falling locks framing a rugged visage. The others similarly were individually distinguished. The legend of the nine hinted at the dark work they had done to found the city, dealings with shadows and spirits that had aided in their prosperity. Similar carved busts in other buildings, and statues of the nine placed throughout Irukad, likewise remained disregarded by the busy citizens of the city, who took no pride in them.

Edrion stood now to deal with the gray man. Virissa rose, as well, casting a last look at the beauty across the room, then followed him toward this sour-faced man. Familiar with the legends, Edrion made a sign to his god, a small circle and two lines in the air—the sun and its rays—as he glanced at the nine busts.

The old man in gray watched carefully as the pair approached, pushing through the crowd. He saw a tall, dark-haired woman in a leather tunic bossed with iron and worn leather pants and boots with a longsword at her side and a commanding attitude, just as Edrion had described her. A pale scar running the length of her right cheek identified her as one to contend with, should that be required. A free sword, and a free woman besides, beholden to no one and no army, no corps, no lord or king. And dangerous, thereby.

But no more dangerous than Edrion, the bearded, handsome blond northron in his plain tunic and boots and with his well-worn sword and knives, a displaced son of money and likely of good training, surely, and free himself to follow whatever paths the gods put him on.

Both wore on their belts full purses, but surely not filled with gold or silver, only what they needed to get by on the road. Alone in the world, then, the both of them. A long time homeless, and Edrion cast out by his family, in any event, for one too many indiscretions. Useless to anyone other than for sword work, and useless to each other except as drinking companions and thieves. But dangerous, yes, of course, and necessary for this gray stranger from the dark temple, so long as they understood that he, too, was dangerous, as well as a willing bargainer. Edrion had agreed to their contract; all that remained was to complete it. A short walk to the old temple that frightened so many but held its secrets well, and so, be done with it.

"I will show you the way," the gray man said, gesturing, and led them from the loud public house into the street.

As crowds pushed by them under the few torches lighting their way, Virissa asked their guide, "Does Edrion trust you on this?"

"Why not ask him?"

Edrion told Virissa, "For this night, yes. There's gold in it for us, and little work to do. Deliver what this one gives us at the temple."

"The scroll," said the swordswoman.

"And wicked it is," Edrion told her. "I would not dare this but for the money. The scroll is a danger."

"It calls up demons? Unseats kings?"

"It is Death itself," Edrion told her.

Virissa made a sound. "You should have told me so before I agreed to this. 'Death itself.' What have you done, Edrion?"

The gray man, turning his head to watch them as they walked, said, "It teaches of death in all its dimensions. Death can be a living thing in itself. It will be worth the risk."

Virissa made another sound and looked up, regarding the night sky. "I *will* say that you picked a splendid night for it."

"You mean the moon," said the gray man.

"Exactly."

The old moon, so called, was the dark moon at certain seasons, so unshining and cold that it made the streets no brighter than the tunnels of a tomb—perfect for thieving in the shadows but making for a cursed night, many felt. An old sentiment. Superstition, nothing more.

"Moon or no moon, we're in it now," Edrion told her. "You like to eat, do you not? Tell her, you."

He meant the tall gray man.

Virissa said, "You don't even know his name!" And to their guide: "Do you have a name?"

"Names are not needed in transactions such as ours. But the gold will be paid if you succeed."

"Just make sure the coins are gold and not brass," Virissa warned him, and to Edrion: "Like Milissia last year."

"He fooled us both," Edrion reminded her. "A simple error made in the rush of the moment."

The gray man let out a muffled chuckle. "We all serve the same master, do we not? We know the truth. Coin. The world is made for the rich."

Before Virissa could offer a witty or vulgar response, from across the street, a short, weighty young man hailed Edrion, waving and calling his name.

Virissa said, "He knows you."

"Ignore him."

"Why?"

The short, weighty young man went on his way, shrugging off Edrion's dismissal of him.

"It's not him so much as his family."

"Ah."

"They're crude. They don't treat him well at all."

"But they have money," said Virissa, "by the looks of that fine attire."

"They do."

"Then he and his fine attire should be careful walking the streets in this part of town."

The tall man said, "And he'd best be good with that sword of his."

"He is, actually," Edrion allowed. "His appearance is deceptive."

"True of so much in this world," said their guide. "We are here, Edrion."

They had passed under an ancient stone arch overgrown with moss and vines visible even in the dull light the night allowed them and were now in a small courtyard shouldered on two sides by old stone walls upon which sat statues, half the size of humans, of what appeared to be demons or gargoyles. Ahead were wide stairs leading into the structure itself, an abandoned temple with little indication of the god or goddess it had been built to honor.

Virissa said, "We're in the oldest part of the city."

"We are," said the nameless gray robe. "This temple was built when Irukad was a place of mud huts and fisherfolk. It is part temple, part tomb. It housed the spirits of the monsters that owned this land. It was built to placate them. Allow the people here to build their lives free of evil."

"By the manner of the city now," Virissa said, "they were not entirely successful."

The gray robe released a sound of mirth. "Even so. We human beings are as capable of evil as any demons and dark gods, are we not?"

Virissa asked him, "Did they placate those spirits by sacrificing some of themselves on nights such as this?"

"They did," said the robe. "A custom abandoned when the temple was."

Irritated, Edrion said, "Can we get on with it?"

"We can, my friend." The gray man nodded succinctly. "I will now enter this place. Remain here but a few moments and I shall return with the scroll, as we agreed. Then you can deliver it to Lord Masor."

Edrion told him, "We'll accompany you."

"We prefer to remain by your side at all times," said Virissa. "The three of us being human and all, and as capable of evil as demons."

Once more, that muffled sound of mirth. "You may if you wish. The way is dark but known to me, so stay close."

He moved across the courtyard and up the wide steps, then through one of the tall doorways from which the doors had long since fallen away. Inside, Edrion and Virissa listened to the soft bootsteps of their guide and the sound of his robe moving in the darkness until both noises went silent. They stopped where they were.

"He's gone ahead of us," Edrion said.

Virissa gripped her sword and freed that weapon halfway from its scabbard. "This is not good for us," she said quietly.

"Do we try to follow him or not?"

"I say we go back to the courtyard. This isn't the smart place for us right now."

"You face front. I'll watch behind us. Back-to-back."

Virissa pulled out her sword. "Listen."

They both heard the sounds all around them—whispering, shuffling, soft sounds of... what? Other priests? Things on the prowl?

"The height of the old moon," Virissa said, "and we're in ruins that are half temple and half tomb."

"Think of the gold."

"Think of our *lives*."

Edrion, sword out and playing the point before him, made the return path through the darkness and into the open, onto the portico of the wide stairs. Neither he nor Virissa sheathed their weapons just yet. They listened for further shuffling and whispering from within the old stone walls.

They heard soft bootsteps, and the tall gray man emerged from the darkness and onto the portico. In his left hand was the scroll protected within a large, open-ended wooden casing, a tube. In his right hand, he held a long knife, simple and efficient in design and dripping blood.

"Imagine my shock," he told Virissa and Edrion, "when I learned that you two had slain the single priest protecting this temple and stolen this scroll from him. What devils you are."

Edrion stated the obvious. "We've been played for fools." To the robe: "Is there even a Lord Masor?"

"He died earlier this evening. Killed in his garden. You two murdered him, as well. I shall have to explain these horrors to the night watch."

Virissa took one step toward him. "No. Now we sword you and take the scroll to sell. Our payment."

The gray man told her, "Do you think me a fool? All unprepared? The watch will find your corpses here. I have my protectors."

Edrion said, "The old things that guard this place."

"Ageless vampires," said the robe. "A family of them." He called out a series of syllables, a command or alert in the language of necromancers and demonologues. In answer, the shuffling in the shadows came to life as dark forms, half the size of any human and squat, but with wide mouths, sharp fangs, useless, atrophied wings on their sides, and talons on both forefeet and rear. Apparent even in the dim moonlight, one betrayed a long streak of white bristly hair along its head.

The face of another protruded in a very long snout and jaw. Some of the others similarly appeared to be deformed.

"Great Krius," Edrion said. "Back away." He moved quickly down the wide steps of the portico, again making that sign before him to his god.

Virissa joined him in the courtyard, where they awaited the hopping things that moved to surround them. Even under the poor light of the old moon, their bright green eyes shone like lamps and their fangs revealed their sharpness.

As the vanguard of the things, three of them, came close, Edrion called out, "Now!" and opened the pouch on his belt.

Virissa did the same. Each retrieved a handful of powder or grains and pitched them at the three vampires.

The things hissed in response and backed away, cawing and rolling in pain on the flagstones of the courtyard. Mist or smoke came from the three. Two died where they were, stretching out and flattening as though deflated of air, green eyes going as dark as the moon. The third revived and waddled toward Virissa and Edrion, scuttling as well as it could and moving its small wings back and forth in a useless display of ferocity.

"Salt!" the gray man called out.

Edrion yelled at him, "Do you think us fools? All unprepared?"

The crippled thing was now joined by the remainder of its family, seven of the vampires, which moved to encircle Virissa and Edrion.

The two moved back-to-back, turning together to confront whichever of the things would come at them first.

One of the largest of them jumped toward Virissa, who cast salt at it, blinding it. It mewled and fell away, scraping at its face

with a clawed forepaw, while another moved in, undeterred.

Edrion, however, faced three of the things. They hopped to confront him at once. He cast salt at them as they came forward, and one puled and screed as the salt bit into it. But the other two evaded the swordman's cast and jumped at him.

Edrion grunted, swinging his sword and catching one of them, which let out a dark liquid, blood or whatever was in these damnable things. The other caught Edrion by the leg, clamping its jaws, crippling him. He fell onto his free knee, which brought the wounded one at him as quickly as it could manage. It hopped onto Edrion, catching him by the shoulder. He fell, making small sounds and struggling with his left hand to retrieve salt in his defense.

Virissa half-turned to witness what had happened. She yelled now to the gray man, "Call them off!"

He laughed at her. "I cannot! You brought this on yourselves!"

Virissa threw a cloud of salt at another of the things that approached her, then faced two more, almost the last of them. But she was distracted, hearing no sound from Edrion.

The two things atop him, however, now moved to either side of her to attack her next.

"Call them off!"

It was a new voice, unknown to Virissa and coming from the portico, from behind the gray man.

"Call them off now, priest, or join them!"

Looking up, Virissa caught a glimpse of someone behind the gray robe, a short someone with sword point placed directly between the robe's shoulders.

The priest hesitated only a moment, then called out further arcane syllables.

Virissa stood panting, sweating in the night, sword still at the ready, watching as the things around her slowly backed away, clawed feet clacking on the stones, the wounded of them mewling as they pulled away.

"Walk!"

It was the short man again, ordering the robe to move down the steps of the portico and through the shuffling crowd of demons.

Virissa shoved her sword into its scabbard and turned immediately to Edrion, who lay motionless behind her, with not even a groan coming from him. She felt him and then saw the blood pooling beneath him. She dug her hands into his tunic, rocking him to revive him.

"Get up, Edrion! Stay here! By Hesta, *don't you die*!" And then, with all the ferocity within her, to the priest, "Help him! *Bring him back*!"

The short man behind him said, "Do it, monster. The scroll. Give it to her."

"I can say a command to kill you with it while I hold it."

"Then you die before you begin those words."

"And who are you to understand what is in this scroll?"

"But I do. Now give it to her." And when the priest hesitated: "Now, Ata!"

So he did have a name. He grumbled, swearing something unintelligible, but then cast the casement at Virissa. It landed on the stones before her, making a cracking sound. She grabbed the tube and reached inside one open end with her fingers, pulling free a scroll of old skin.

"Unroll it," said the short man behind the robe.

Virissa said to him, "You're his friend. The one we saw on the street."

"The same. Unroll the book and place it atop him. That's the best we can hope for." And he ordered the priest, "Tell her the words to say or within one breath, I promise you, you'll be in Hell with everyone else you've ever cheated in this world. Speak!"

Ata did so, and a change came over the short man as he heard the words. He watched as the priest moved away from his sword point and turned to face him.

Virissa saw it and called out, "Strike him!"

The short man tried to do so, but his arm was numb.

Ata laughed at him. "While the scroll lives, I am empowered. Shall I make you stab yourself with your own weapon?"

"Stop it!" Virissa yelled and reached into her pouch.

Ata said to her, "More salt? To what effect? It cannot harm me, woman."

"Not for you!"

She withdrew a sharp stone, a gleaming gem, and cast it directly at the unmoving short man, who grunted in fear. But the gem did not strike him. Within that heartbeat, as it reached him, a mist appeared about him, then vanished as the gem dropped to the stones.

"Whose knowledge is this?" Ata yelled at Virissa.

Immediately the short man was moving forward, and the point of his blade pierced Ata's heavy robe, cutting into him. The priest grimaced and swore. He placed his hands over the wound, and the hands went wet with blood.

"A powerful stone?" the short man asked Virissa.

"From years ago. A witch we met. Now help me, priest!"

"Do it!" commanded the short man. "And no tricks this time!"

Ata did it, looking down at his dark, wet hands, speaking the syllables. Virissa repeated the words and tones, then yelled at Edrion again.

"Wake up, damn you! Your time is not yet!"

"Fools," said Ata. And to the swordsman before him: "Who are you to understand such things?"

"My father empowered you. You don't remember?"

"You are Malon."

"I am."

Grunting in discomfort, Ata told him, "Your father was a great man to assist us in maintaining this old temple. The dark gods welcomed him when he died."

"When you and your kind killed him. If Edrion does not revive, priest, you will do everything in your power to bring him back. Or I will. Your life for his."

But a groan came from Edrion as Virissa repeated the incantation as well as she could. Somewhere, shapes or forms or shadows hanging nearby in the night heard her and acted, so that Edrion's bleeding stopped, and he moaned, then tried to move.

Virissa helped him up. The scroll dropped to the flags.

Edrion whispered dryly, "A... dream."

"And quite a dream!" Virissa laughed, steadying him as he rocked on his feet.

"I'm all right now," he told her.

"No, you're not. Move slowly." She held him strongly and stared into his eyes, studying him. "What did you see?" she whispered.

"Darkness. Shapes. Memories. And, I think... the god of shadows. *His* dark god!"—meaning Ata.

"You're not ready to die yet, Edrion."

"I am not, Virissa."

She retrieved his sword and handed it to him. "Can you see me? Know where we are?"

"That damned gray man and his vampires."

"Which we defeated by the help of your friend."

Edrion looked at the priest and saw Malon behind him. "You made it here."

"A bit late, I fear," said the short man.

"This was a *plan*?" Virissa

said sharply. "Edrion! You didn't tell me?"

Still wakening, he told her, "We didn't know... whether this priest had spies or shadows about. I... didn't dare."

"It's the truth," said Malon.

"Wise of you," said Ata. "I was indeed trying to watch you from my place." He looked down at his wet hands with concern. If he had been attempting to stop the bleeding, he had not been successful.

"Another good reason to kill you," Virissa said in anger. "Do it now, friend Malon, or allow me the honor!"

"Let his own demons do it," said the short man. "Have you steel and flint?"

"Right here." Virissa retrieved them from her pouch.

"Strike fire to the scroll," Malon told her. "My mother and I begged my father to destroy the thing. This one hid it away"— meaning Ata.

Virissa said, "Let us sell it, at least."

Malon shook his head. "Too dangerous for anyone to handle. Trust me. Burn it."

Virissa looked to Edrion, who nodded.

But Ata, managing himself despite his wound, called out words, and in response, the scroll moved, attempting like some awkward, peculiar worm to hunch its way free, crawling and rolling.

"Stop it!" called Malon.

Virissa stepped down with one boot to trap the thing, then knelt to it. Holding the flint under one edge of the scroll, she struck with the steel.

Ata cried out, "Do not! It is the last of them! It is a *holy thing*! *Do not!*"

But already the old skin had taken the sparks. Virissa stepped back. Flames pulled across it and sent stinking black smoke into the sky to obscure the old moon. Virissa thought she heard faint voices nearby, those things aware in the night, making sounds as the scroll died and took its evil with it.

"What have you done?" said Ata.

"What was needed long ago," Malon told him. "Now give me your purse. The gold."

"Gold!" said the priest, taking the full pouch from his belt and handing it to Malon with a bloody hand. "I command shadows and see through time, and on this, our holy day of the dark moon, you still want *gold*!"

Malon took the pouch and tossed it to Edrion, then said to Ata, "You'll command your shadows soon enough. Back inside with you to those things you awakened. They still hunger for human blood, I'm sure—yours, if there's anything human left to you. You've brought this on yourself."

Ata said nothing. He was shivering now.

Edrion said to him, "You must know *some* words, at least, to save yourself, or at least attempt it. It's your holy day."

The priest pulled in a breath and looked up at the moon and the old stars around it, as if contemplating how they might assist him, or even that he, as small as he was and within the shadows of the earth, should die here in this way beneath the old moon.

He said something Malon heard and did not understand.

"Walk," said Edrion's friend, pushing with the sword.

The old man did so, across the portico and into the dark temple, trailing blood and reciting loudly syllables only sorcerers would know.

Malon waited, lest Ata attempt by some trick to escape into the night.

Virissa and Edrion did not move.

From within the temple then came the priest's failing voice in echoes of agony—the howls of a man doomed of soul being eaten alive by the monsters he himself had called forth.

From where he stood, Malon heard the noises of the feast. He held back the need to retch but retrieved Virissa's jewel. Then he hurried down the steps of the temple, putting away his sword.

"Holy Krius," whispered Edrion, staring at the portico.

There, in the dull light, they saw a vampire scurry onto the stones, chasing one of Ata's arms... or legs, and catching hold of it in its jaws as a second monster hurried out to steal it for itself. The torn limb flailed weakly, partly alive and fighting to escape even as the two vampires growled like dogs competing for a bone, before the first clawed the second, which turned and scurried into the temple again.

Then the first sat on the portico in the darkness and chewed on whatever it was that had been of the sorcerer.

"Wine," said Malon, turning away. "Or cold brew. Anything to wash away these horrors."

Edrion scabbarded his blade and, still weak, stepped ahead to give his friend a great hug in thanks. "How shall I repay you?"

Malon grinned. "That is something I shall seriously need to consider!"

Virissa put away her own sword and accepted her gem from Malon. "Your father in association with the priests of this temple?"

Malon shrugged. "They helped him make his fortune. In return, he assisted them, particularly in preventing the politicians of this hellhole of a city from interfering with his work."

"As ever," said Virissa. "That is my understanding of politicians and priests. I prefer common tavern owners."

"Then let's get that brew," said Edrion. "I am well enough now."

"Goddess knows how I feared

for you," said Virissa. "I should have given my own life. It means little."

"It means much to me," Edrion told her, meaning it. "I cannot face the world without you."

"Then we'll continue to face it together. And with this good sword alongside us."

As they made their way back into the lighted streets, Malon said, "Allow this good sword to show you the way to a *decent* house with *decent* brew!"

"In this town?" said Virissa.

A few nights later, Virissa and Edrion sat at the same table they had shared the night Ata had come to them and led them nearly to their deaths. The same crowd, the same noises, the same brew of questionable satisfaction but sufficient to relax them, all the same. Then Edrion stood and dropped a few coppers onto the stained tabletop.

"So soon?" Virissa said to him.

"One last night with Malon," he explained, "before we leave."

"Your heavy friend who surprised me so. Fortunate that he was there."

"He is fortunate in other ways. Did I tell you that half his weight is below his belt?"

"A prize for you, then."

"Indeed." Edrion looked about the public house. "I'm sorry that we don't see her."

"Just another dream that might have been," said Virissa. "There have been so many."

"The stables, then, tomorrow."

She lifted her gourd of beer and ducked her head. "Back on the road we go."

She watched as her friend made his way to the open door of the house. As he glanced at the nine wooden busts above him, Edrion shivered and again drew the sign of his god in the air. Against the crowd in the door-way, a giant pushed his way past him, followed by a lovely young woman with red hair, perfect cheekbones, beautiful eyes. She followed the giant into the crowded room, and he made space at a table for her to sit.

Virissa followed her with her gaze, thanking the goddess for her good luck. She glanced back at Edrion.

He smiled at her and gestured with one hand as though he had managed magically to make this beauty appear again on earth.

Virissa looked at the young woman, who held her in her gaze, as well.

Beautiful young woman.

Seduce her?

Or take the bauble that rested at her throat, a gem surely worth a small fortune?

As steadily as she could, Virissa got to her feet, dropped a few coppers onto the stained tabletop, and began to make her way across the crowded room.

Baubles could wait.

ABOUT THE AUTHOR

David C. Smith (he/him, born August 10, 1952, in Youngstown, Ohio) is the author of 28 novels and numerous short stories, many of them part of his ongoing Attluman cycle, which features his Sword & Sorcery protagonist Oron. With Richard L. Tierney, he wrote the Red Sonja series of fantasy novels. Smith won the 2018 Atlantean Award from the Robert E. Howard Foundation for Outstanding Achievement, Book, for *Robert E. Howard: A Literary Biography*. He lives in Palatine, Illinois, with his wife, Janine, and their daughter, Lily.

davidcsmith.net

The Beast of the Shadow Gum Trees

by T.K. Rex

One

The Women of the Waves

And so Moth buried Amas with his lute beneath their favorite lilac tree, and willed himself to die beside him. His cells refused, for he had given up all but the magic he had started with irrationally long ago, in exchange for one last chance at love.

He stumbled to the edge of the Neonate Sea, and gave himself to the green waves, where the serpent-tailed women of the water greeted him with sympathy and sea grass braids.

"Let me drown," he begged them.

"But you cannot die," they sang.

"I can. I can now."

"What of your forest? What of the land you tend?"

"I've looked after it for longer than your sea has been a sea. It has maintained without me for the dozen years I've been a mortal man, and will maintain a thousand more alone, until another like me comes along. Now let me drown, I'm tired, and I should have listened to my listlessness and decomposed before Amas sang me that wretched song." And at that last, he wept, because the song had been the thing that made him fall in love.

A song for the lonely creature of the lilac wood.

The humans of his continent had called him many things across the generations since they'd built their towns. Tree's Vengeance, Spidertender, Man of the Mushrooms. The One Who Weaves Variance. Guardian of the Land.

None had called him lonely.

But he had been. And he hadn't known.

"You're not yourself, old friend," the oldest of the sea-folk said. "Let us help you start again, carry you to a new shore."

"You'll do what you will when I can swim no more, but please, if you have been my friend at all these hundred thousand years, you'll let me drown."

Moth pushed past her, deep into the cool green waves, and when his boots no longer touched the sand, he dove, and swam.

In floating dreams, he felt Amas's fingers intertwine with his.

"What will the villagers think, when you bring home a husband made of mushrooms and moss?"

Amas smiled like the sunlight glinting off the summer stream, and said, "We'll tell them it's a fashion from a foreign land! I'll make it a song. Before you know it, we'll all wear twigs in our hair."

Moth smiled softly. "Most of them are not as kind as you."

Amas shrugged, and fiddled with the leaf he'd been about to tuck behind his ear.

"But I may have another way..." Moth mused. Some like him could change their form at will, like Shaktakash. Perhaps he could remake himself, grow old like humans do... he had been tired for a long time, after all...

He dreamt, too, of Shaktakash, whom he had loved so long ago, before the valley rift grew wide enough to make the sea, and she stayed with the other shore. Such was the nature of their chosen role, to space themselves throughout the continents, maintaining the diversity of living forms.

In his dream, she walked a desert road, between two fields of shattered swords.

And night became dawn in a slow gray descent, as the women of the water carried Moth past silent shipwrecks to a strange and distant shore.

Where yellow sand fought slate-gray waves, the women whispered to his salt-wet ears, "May you find new verdure here." And with six gentle kisses

and a fading song, they slipped beneath the foam, and they were gone.

Two

A Foreign Forest's War

A steep cliff lined the beach, its height unknown above the fog. He placed a hand against the yellow stone and felt the former sand, the threads of fungus, and the tittering of roots and burrowers above. No rain had fallen here for months. No standing water but the sea.

He found a narrow path, worn by some animal as wide as him with hooves, and climbed, and climbed.

He unwove the green-brown seaweed from his auburn hair and pulled a stray fish scale from his ear. His sopping mushroom leather boots collected sand enough to almost turn to stone, and his layered tunics clung to his cold-roughened skin. His breath and heartbeat quickened as he climbed, and he felt the full thirst of his days at sea. He drank what he could from the fog, through his tanned and reddened skin, and climbed until strange succulents loomed through the gray.

When the ground was finally flat and birdsongs he had never heard before filled up the fog, a grove of tall trees loomed ahead, unlikely in their common height. A planted grove? Perhaps their fruit or seeds were ripe this time of year, and he could make a meal.

The birds began to quiet at the line of trees. There was no underbrush, no groundcover, just fallen, grayish, sickle leaves. The trunks were multicolored under bark they shed in strips and the branches bore no fruit. Small cone-shaped seed pods poked his soles, so hard and dense whatever tiny morsel grew inside would be a pyrrhic victory. Perhaps the people here had ways

...but no. No birds, nor land-bound foragers in sight. Only small black ants crawled up and down the loose, pale bark between dark sores that oozed an oily red sap.

He ate as many ants as he could stand, and wondered, briefly, if the women of the waves could carry him to some more fruitful land. But to die here as a starving wanderer, he mused, might be a fitting end.

Between the rows of trees, a shadow in the mist—a dark, hulking goat? Perhaps an elk? But no, it had a single spiral horn, held high and sharp, and eyes—as it turned its head to meet his cautious gaze—eyes glowing fiercely red through the ambient, thick gray.

He stopped, and placed a hand against the nearest tree. It knew the beast, and loathed him.

He felt the creature's gaze crawl up his spine. *Leave, human.* The silent voice scraped through his mind like living meat across a field of rusty knives.

"I have nowhere else to go," Moth said.

LEAVE.

What power did this elaphine monstrosity possess? The tree beneath his palm was inarticulate with fear and rage.

The mammal snorted, stomped a cloven hoof against the dust and sickle leaves, and aimed his long black horn at him.

The eyes... the red eyes...

A wave of nausea came over Moth and he bent, hands to his knees. The forest swirled with black spots around the edges of the gray. He coughed, and cursed, and looked up just in time to see the elk-beast charge, faster with a smoother gait than any deer.

He tumbled more than dodged, fell hard on the dry ground, hit an elbow on a rock and felt the shooting pain. He pushed himself into an awkward kneel just as the angry creature turned to aim at him again.

With both palms against the ground, Moth called to the mycelium beneath. It was weakened beyond helping him, all through the floor of this cursed wood. Even if it could, it whispered, it would not, for it was siding with the animal intent on his demise.

Why?

No time for an answer—he tried to dodge the horn again, but, this time, he was not so quick. It grazed his arm and searing pain shot through the limb. He cried out and held the bloody wound through his torn tunic sleeve.

"Wait, please—" what other recourse did he have but pleading, now? How much he'd given up, and in the end, for what?

When the deer-brute didn't pause, but aimed to charge again, Moth grasped out for the closest tree.

A heinous crack, the weakened wood contorting, bark peeling and unpeeling to align itself against his skin, ants startled into chaos, thin legs stuck where sticky blood soaked through. The tree pulled him close and armored him.

The one-horned beast stopped then, and laughed, a laughter like a thousand silent, giant frogs at night.

Ah. I've seen your kind of sorcery before. Show me why you're here.

Before Moth had a chance to speak, the scab of memory was ripped from him, hoisted by red eyes into the creature's black abyss:

An echo of ages alone with the land.

Amas smiling, hand on his hand.
Their tangled sheets of spider silk.
A song meant only for his ears,
a dying gasp,
and then the cool green waves.

The villainous beast shook his silver-streaked mane and growled across Moth's mind, *Ah. You left your land behind for love, and then to die. You selfish fool.*

Amas's face, so close to his, the hand, alive, so fresh from violated memory Moth's fingers tingled underneath the bark and blood.

He fell into the sickle leaves, and sobbed until the guilt could let him up for air. Cold sweat covered him beneath the bark, and ants were crawling on his eyelids, in his nose, trapped and writhing in his streams of snot and tears.

Do you still want your mortal death?

The creature's eyes burned into him with a simmering red glare. The single horn, held at an angle, dripped a single drop of blood. His blood. It fell onto a sickle leaf, red against orange-gray.

While the beast stood waiting, Moth spoke to the mycelia. "Why side with this creature? What has he done for you? What has he done to the trees?"

Whispered giggles through the hyphae *Answer the question.*

Did Moth still want his mortal death? Of course he did. He still wanted to grow old with Amas, tend their garden, listen to his songs change subtly as his voice grew deep with age. Even immortality would be more kind, if the land below Moth's feet contained the remnants of his bones. But even hyphae cannot stretch across the sea.

And so, what was the point of death? He could have argued with the women of the waves until they let him drown, but silence, too, is choice.

"I don't know."

The creature huffed, and shook his black and silver mane again, and said, *Walk with me.*

Moth tried to stand, but stumbled, and fell back to his knees. The creature waited as he coaxed what little help he could from the reluctant ground. He let his armor fall, asked the ants, who could, to leave, and stood.

He walked beside the beast into the slowly thinning fog. His shoulder was as tall as Moth, and dark as a new moon.

There was a raven with your power here. The power you gave up for love. She left to stop the war. The creature gestured at the forest with his horn and said, *All this was chaparral, back then. Scrub oak, pine and cactus, creosote and sage.*

"You should stay out of other people's memories."

A snort, the slightest drooping of the head. *Perhaps nothing's happened to your lilac wood since you deserted it, but my chaparral was not so fortunate. When the raven left, the warring humans tore the ground to plant these trees, so they could build enormous weapons, fortresses and ships.*

"Surely you could fight them off? You could have killed me easily."

I was more timid then. And ignorant.

The creature stopped to scrape his horn against a healthy trunk. The red sap beaded at the cut.

These trees are from another land, like you. They're thirsty here, and weak, and their wood turned out to be too fragile for the purposes of war.

"I can relate."

When I realized that the raven wasn't coming back, I slowly learned how I could help the chaparral regrow.

He saw it now. The length and angle of the scratch resembled all the older, gaping wounds across the trees. "A plague. You're spreading it." Moth felt the nausea return. "That's why this forest hates and fears you."

Does it? I suppose it would. But look. The trees were smaller, denser up ahead. *The plague is not enough. New trees still sprout around the edges of the grove. Even the young shoots are inedible to all the grazers here, and as they grow, their shade prevents the chaparral from flowering. The birds have less to eat each year and I fear the trees will spread across the land in time, replacing everything with their monotony.*

Moth took it in, this battle-field where rival ecosystems fought. He'd lived long enough to see entire landscapes come and go, the species on them change, the weather shift and mountains rise. "If your raven can, I'm sure she'll return to help the land adjust."

She's been gone more than a hundred years.

Moth sat on the nearest fallen log. His hunger slowed his wits, or perhaps it was the loss of blood. He placed a palm against the log, and felt for any hyphae in the rot—there were none. The wood was alien enough not even this land's fungus could make use of it. No wonder the mycelia had sided with the beast.

"What do you want from me?"

You could relearn your power. Kill the trees. Help me regrow the chaparral.

"Even if it worked like that, I have no interest in returning to that role. I was tired of it long before I threw myself into the sea."

Then you are a selfish fool.

Moth shook his head. His arm ached badly and his focus wavered. He blinked away the blurriness and said, "Why don't you learn how? You're just as capable as me."

I'm not opposed. But I would need someone to teach me.

"The first of us figured it out on their own."

And how long did that take? My kind live long, but not forever.

Instead of answering, Moth slid onto the forest floor so he could lean against the fallen trunk.

This, perhaps, was death approaching. Another chance. This time, saying nothing would be a different choice entirely. Perhaps he only wanted what was easiest.

Moth.

"You don't get to use my name," he slurred. "You never asked for it."

The creature knelt in front of him, black and muscular and sharp, chest heavy in the sickle leaves. Its red eyes blurred.

You're right. My name is Selapon. Had the creature's voice gone gentle, or was it simply fading off, into the distance...

Selapon nudged him in the knee with the soft tip of his nose. Moth blinked and for a moment, met his eyes. They were merely reddish-brown, not glowing anymore.

Use my magic. Heal yourself.

Amas. Shaktakash. The lilac wood. All the loves come and gone, entire landscapes buried under stone, subducted deep inside the world's heart. To take on one more place would mean to fall in love again, and that would mean to lose it all, again. Again.

"No," he whispered, and the forest floor approached his head, and he felt dry leaves against his cheek.

And noon became night in a long wash of scarlet and gold.

Moth woke in the dust to the song of crickets and frogs, and the light of a full moon just past the cactus pads above.

He thought of fireflies, and of Amas, and of the forest that he'd lost, and if only, if only he'd kept his full power, he would have known the plague was coming, could have made the village more prepared. No one should have to die that way.

He had been selfish.

He curled up to cry into his knees, and noticed that his arm was mostly healed.

A name... he'd heard the creature give its name...

"Selapon!" he yelled into the night. A startled sleeping bird nearby took flight.

Leave if you wish. The beast emerged from the shadows of the brush as Moth sat up. *It was the ground that staved off death for you, not I.*

"You dragged me out of the forest."

I didn't want to smell your corpse around the trees I'm trying to kill.

Moth stood, and dusted off his now-dry clothes, and walked on into the chaparral.

Three
A Long-Tailed Raven

And night gave way to dawn again three times as he walked on. The chaparral thinned out to scattered brush and bare rock, and then he found a road, and followed it, and wished for a good meal and a bed. Something in him grew more certain than it ever had, that this was the right choice, to suffer the remainder of his mortal life, however sad.

The light grew low and gold as he approached a town. Perhaps they'd have a beer, or mead, or some unlikely local brew. Perhaps a garden he could tend. Perhaps a lilac tree.

Under orange and scarlet clouds, the ruined town came fully into view. Charred stone and splintered wood, ground stained and strewn with broken swords.

A long-tailed raven, with wing feathers on its legs, flew up to him and perched atop the barren rib of some poor ungulate left rotting on the road.

It bared the pointed teeth inside its beak and spoke—a gravel voice, a raven's voice, articulated in a way no raven would have time to learn. "Moth."

Of course it would be her. "Shaktakash."

"I didn't know our kind could give our power up."

"I heard you tried to stop this war. Looks like it didn't go so well."

The black bird cocked her head, spread four wings out to fly, and in a swirled sunset breeze, collapsed into a human form. He'd never learned that trick.

"How long has it been?" She asked, voice smooth and intimate, as if they'd seen each other yes-

terday. She wore robes as dark and dusty as they'd always been, and mycelia like spiderwebs across her redwood skin, white hair in many braids pulled back into a tree-branch ring.

"Long enough entire stars have died."

"Did you ever find out what they are?"

"A bard told me they're fireflies."

"I see."

And there they were again, the tears that couldn't stop, as if his eyes had soaked up the entire sea on his way here.

And the woman he'd loved long ago held out her arms for him, and held him until his shaking stopped, and finally, softly, said, "I felt you in the shadow gum grove. I thought for sure you'd help the unicorn."

He shook his head. "If I merged again with the mycelia, I'd lose the cells that knew his cells, the skin that touched his skin."

"A man you lost? The bard?"

"His name was Amas."

They built a fire upwind of the ruined town, and shared what little scraps of food were left from the abandoned stores. He told her everything that Selapon had stolen from his mind, and it was the first time he told the story willingly, and it hurt to do, but it felt good.

She listened. Through his long pauses and his intermittent sobs. And when the story had been told enough that crickets gave away the end, she said, "It was not your fault, you know. The plague."

"If I had the power to prevent it, and did not, it was."

"You didn't have the power at the time."

"But I knew that it would come, eventually. Something always does. I should have found another to replace me before giving up my role."

"Perhaps." She sighed, and

looked into the distance at the ruined town. The songs of twilight insects filled the space left by her voice. They were upwind of the ash and rotting flesh, so the only odor on the evening air came from their campfire of juniper, and the fragrant sage around them when the breeze danced by. "I wish I could go back," she finally said.

"To the—what did you call him—*unicorn*?"

She nodded. "I left to stop the war, but my negotiations failed. I didn't understand what I do now."

"That humans die no matter what you do?"

She looked at him, with sympathetic crinkles in the corners of her eyes. "That the scale of things has changed. The rate of new inventions has begun to build upon itself, and there are humans who believe that power comes from endless growth."

"You've told them that's not how it works."

"They didn't care." He could see the hot frustration in her eyes. "I don't think I can handle this alone."

He shook his head in disbelief. "You? The great Shaktakash Niksa, Guardian of the Towering Redwoods, Song-Keeper of the Day the World Burned, Savior of the Long-Tailed Birds, and Raven of the Chaparral? I'm certain there is nothing you can't do."

She rolled her eyes, but not without a subtle pleasure. "I've been seeking listeners. Like us when we were new. To learn the language of mycelia, maintain the rates of variance, help the landscape survive rapid change. This continent has very few of us, and the generation that taught you and I have merged into the aggregate beyond what I can sense."

The last time Moth had sought an elder, he found only giant mushrooms growing in a ring, deep within the swamps across the plain. He'd seen it as a sign he, too, should find some other thing to be. But he'd been wrong.

A thought occurred to him. "The unicorn seemed interested."

She smiled, unexpectedly. "Did he, now?"

"He wanted to learn how to kill the trees, bring back the chaparral."

"He wasn't ready when I left. He hadn't learned the art of listening."

"It's not his strongest skill."

She laughed.

He very nearly grinned, then sighed, and said, "I suppose you're going to ask me to go back and mentor him."

"If you don't mind a few more years of life. You have so much to teach, Moth, even as a mortal man."

"He needs to understand that nothing goes back to the way it was."

"And that goes for you and I, as well," she said. "We must keep trying the unknown."

He pulled the old refrain from memory, "Because we have no way of knowing what survives an unknown threat."

"So the songs I keep insist." She smiled softly in the firelight, and let the desert insects fill the silence of the night.

Four
Listen

And the desert dawn became orange-tinted noon across the sunbathed chaparral, as Moth approached the grove of shadow gums. This time it was smoke, not fog, that filled the air.

Something terrible had happened since he left. His mortal heartbeat quickened in his chest.

He pulled a scarf of spider silk from the cactus leather bag that Shaktakash had sent him with and covered both his nose and mouth. He kept his distance

from the fire's downwind edge and looked for a way into the trees not yet aflame.

"Selapon!"

No answer from the shadows of the smokey wood.

He held a hand to an infected trunk, where gray flakes of ash stuck in the sticky oil oozing from its wounds. The only words within were *fire, pain*.

He brushed away a patch of sickle leaves and pressed his palm into the yellow dust. The ground replied, *Please help—the oil in the trees has made the fire hot and fast. We're familiar with flame but weren't prepared for this.*

"I'm sorry. I have very little magic left."

Then why have you returned at all? What good are you to us?

Flames licked the fallen leaves nearby, and climbed the hanging strips of bark into the trees. He had to move on, quick.

"Tell the burrowers to share their burrows with whoever fits, and pull as many seeds in with them as they can. Anyone too big who cannot make it to the beach will be safest if they stay close to the ground, between the succulents."

Thank you. Find Selapon, he needs your help as well. He fled toward the cliffs.

He thanked the hyphae, wiped off the muddy mix of sweat and dust across his palm, and stood.

A nearby tree on fire burst with a horrendous crack of sound, pelting him with glowing splinters.

He ran west, out of the grove, until his mortal lungs were strained. He caught his breath beneath a twisted pine and yelled out, "Selapon!"

Leave. The voice inside his head this time was weak as sand. He followed it into a patch of spiny succulents with bright red fruit.

I said leave. Why don't you listen?

There, in the shadows, lay the

unicorn. His head against the ground, mane singed, horn charred to a dull point.

"I should have," Moth said, and knelt. Selapon's red eyes squinted, and he wheezed, a sound like wind through leafless trees. "Listened, that is. Not left."

Your enlightenment is late.

"Perhaps. Can you still stand?"

What does it matter? I've destroyed my land.

"What happened?"

I was a fool. I found a human campsite on the beach last night. While they slept, I stole a burning branch of driftwood from their fire and carried it back to the wood, where its ember set the fallen leaves on fire. It was a perspicacious plan: to burn the shadow gums, and let the fire-hardy native plants fill in.

Selapon wheezed, and whimpered.

"It's not what I'd have done, but I'll admit it was clever plan."

It didn't go so well. The gum trees burn so hot the fire turned the scrub oaks and the succulents to ash. It spread to the arroyos before dawn and now more chaparral is ruined than before. I've only made things worse.

Selapon shuddered, and cried out with a haunting, elk-like moan.

"You're in pain. Are you burned?"

It doesn't matter. Go home to your husband's bones. Forget this dying place, and die where you were happiest while it still looks like home.

"Let me see your wounds."

Instead of showing him, the unicorn cried out in pain again, a scream that echoed through the drifting smoke.

Moth felt the ground, asked the mycelia for what the unicorn would not reveal. Against the sandy earth, all along his side, his flesh leaked fluid in a quantity that cactus roots could drink.

Selapon would die and Moth did not have magic to repair his cells.

Just like Amas.

If only Moth had stayed to help when he was asked.

If only he'd stayed in his lilac wood, with his foxes, ferns and spiders.

But there were other ways than magic to address a burn. He shook off his despair as best he could, and said to the mycelia, "Spiders. Bring spiders. Quick."

How many? it replied.

"All of them."

And a long, red-glowing night became gray fog and ash as the sun went round the world one more time.

Four cloven hooves, two mushroom leather boots stepped through the ash that had once been the shadow gums, that had once been the chaparral, that had once been the land Moth knew across the sea, before the rift grew wide and deep enough to let the water in.

Selapon stepped slowly, carefully, between the trunks, black as his fur, save for his left side swathed in spider silk. Moth scanned the ground for signs of life.

At least the shadow gums are finally dead.

Moth placed a hand against a charcoal trunk, to see if Selapon was right.

A whisper, still, of life... a bud below the bark... the satisfaction of a victory. But how...? "What have you done?" he asked the tree.

Just watch, it said, too smug for anything that looked so dead. *You'll see.*

He knelt to touch the ground, careful to avoid the embers in the ash. And he could feel them all across the forest floor—the seeds. The seeds in cone-shaped pods so hard no animal could break them, split willingly by heat, already germinating underneath the ash. All healthy, eager, ready to remake the land before the creosote or oaks could even get a start.

What is it? Selapon asked.

Something's wrong.

Moth shook his head, brushed off his hand, and frowned.

No. Not even this could kill them?! It was all for nothing! He stomped a hoof, then cried aloud in pain.

Moth paused, and thought, and finally said, "Not true. This is the perfect practice ground."

For what?

"For variance. Come, feel this trunk. Not with your horn this time, but with your skin."

Cautiously, Selapon touched his nose to the black bark.

"Inside, what do you feel?"

Hungry.

"Inside the *tree*, Selapon. Listen to it."

This is why you're always touching things? You hear voices through your skin?

"There are intelligences all around us that cannot be seen, or heard. Only invited."

I've seen Shaktakash bend rainstorms to her will, force fish to strand themselves along the shore, make a field of flowers bloom in every color I can see. You're telling me it all comes down to... listening?

"I am."

Selapon was quiet, then, and closed his eyes, and pressed his nose harder into the tree. He stood like that until Moth wondered if he slept.

You're right. It's not a voice, exactly, but it... feels. And yes. It hates me.

"How will you change that?"

Selapon backed away from the trunk, and shook out his mane with a huff. *Why should I? I still want it dead.*

"Imagine if the life inside could regrow differently. If every seed below this ash could sprout as something slightly new. You cannot kill them all, but one by one you can encourage them to try a different way, and see what works best over time. The forest that regrows could give us whole new foods, materials, and medicines. And in time, this land-

scape will face change you can't control—what if this grove becomes the only shelter then?"

I think I understand. His nostrils flared in a deep sigh. *I suppose it starts with making peace.*

"And that begins with listening."

And so, they listened.

As the embers cooled, they listened to the ants emerging from the ash, and to the snakes and quails climbing up from burrows they had shared. And as the afternoon fog devoured the last stubborn strands of smoke, they listened to the seeds of the shadow gum trees, ready, like all seeds, to become something new.

ABOUT THE AUTHOR

T. K. Rex (she/they) writes science fiction and fantasy in San Francisco on Ohlone Ramaytush land. She was raised in Northern California and Northwest New Mexico by Wiccan parents of mostly British and Ashkenazi descent. Recently, she attended the Clarion Writers Workshop in San Diego, and has had short fiction published in *Strange Horizons*, *The Molotov Cocktail*, and *Luna Station Quarterly*. You can say hi and keep up with her latest stories on Twitter and Instagram, where she shares photos of San Francisco and retweets dinosaur stuff.

@tharkibo

SO I'M WRITING A NOVEL...

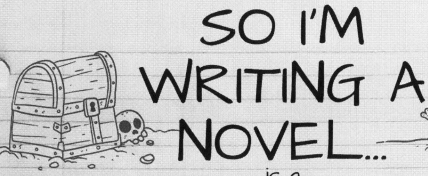

is a
behind-the-scenes podcast,
following the journey
of writing a
SWORD & SORCERY
novel from earliest ideas
all the way through
to publication
and
promotion!

Feat. interviews
with special guests
like
Howard Andrew Jones,
Ngo Vinh-Hoi of
The Appendix N Book Club,
and
Milton Davis.

Find the show at
WWW.SOIMWRITINGANOVEL.COM
and
everywhere
good
podcasts
are
found.

Vapors of Zinai
by J.M. Clarke

The blood of Hori, Terror of Merza, painted the ground in his wake.

Ragged stones sliced bare feet, the pain nigh on unbearable, but bear it he must if he wished to live. Deep rasping breaths spread through the tunnel around him, leaving him glancing back, unsure if they were his or his pursuer's. His heart pounded like a ritual drumbeat in the temple of Priestess Takhat, but he was not in her holy chamber; he was within the blackest caverns beneath Zinai, and they were draped in darkness deeper than Pharaonic tombs.

The Terror of Merza spared no thought for Takhat's handmaiden Bunefer—as much a terror in death as a beauty in life—her final breaths he witnessed by sputtering torchlight. Better she than he, in his mind, even if Takhat would curse his cowardice.

But what could he do? His khopesh was swift and his heart stout, but his pursuer's might was beyond mortality, and it cared naught for the courage of warriors. Only flight would save Hori, but his strength was failing.

And his stalker's endless.

He willed his legs to run. If he could just—

Rounding a corner, the light of the desert moon beckoned in the tunnel's maw. Wild hope sprang up in his breast.

He hobbled on.

Wind tickled his face as the stench of the River of Scales chased away stale air; he had never smelled any scent as sweet.

Then a figure emerged.

Cloaked in shadow, its eyes blazed with hideous vigour.

Hori hesitated, tensed with fear… yet had he been a bit braver, he might have lived. In that heartbeat's pause, his pursuer overtook him. Something forced itself into every pore.

Claws tore at him within until all was blood.

The Terror of Merza fell in a mist of red, his screams buried by the river's roar.

In the moonlight, the figure smiled.

Death hunted Kyembe of Sengezi across the mountains.

Bronze hooves heralded its coming.

Clenching his teeth, the Sengezian scaled a ridge with one arm chafed by rock and the other coiled in burns. Stones slipped between his lean, burnt umber fingers, and dust caked his ring. His sword's ivory hilt dug into his side; if cornered, he would strike these hunters with such fury, his image would live on in their nightmares.

But escaping would be preferable.

Risking a backward glance, he pulled himself onto a ledge; his crimson eyes slid over the road below. Dust clouds churned as four figures rode with a haste born of vengeance; three guards and their incensed master. The wizard Djehuti's emerald eyes glared from within a veil of sheer white cloth, his amber hand gripping his object of power: a hieroglyph-etched horn.

From the tip, a writhing vapour stained the air.

An acrid stink—like oil and brimstone—reached Kyembe and he redoubled his speed; he had witnessed what horrors that gas had wrought.

"Craven thief!" Djehuti cried. "Impotent wizard! Spirit Killer, they call you? Stand, so that I might peel your bones!"

"What fool would listen to such a demand?" Kyembe called back, his rich voice echoing through the peaks. "I am no thief, but you are a cheat. I only took from you what was promised!"

"You slew my guards!" The wizard slid from his mount. His three warriors dismounted, spears at the ready.

Kyembe gave a bitter laugh. "They meant to slay me! What would you have me do, blow them kisses?"

"Try blowing anything when your lungs bubble away," Djehuti growled, shoving his guards forward. "Ready yourselves!"

Words—grating like ground glass—rasped from the wizard's throat; vapour arose from the horn, turning opaque.

Kyembe cursed, dashing along the ledge.

A cascade of pebbles rained down with each footfall, and in his exhaustion, he struggled for balance. The ledge was long and curved away from the road. Perhaps he could lose his pursuers among the rocks.

Kyembe ran on, his slightly pointed ears catching a dull roar. Was that water up ahead? Bare feet pounded on loose stone as a gurgle like bog water crept up the ridge behind him.

He ran faster; danger *might* lay before him, but death definitely lay behind.

Drawing closer to the roar, the ridge abruptly turned.

"No!"

A line of blue thrashed among the rocks far below: the River of Scales.

The ledge ended in mere paces.

Djehuti and his guards drifted toward him, perched on a thick, green cloud as though it were solid ground. The Sengezian's crimson eyes searched the river and the jagged slope above it. Moving back along the ledge, he ducked behind the ridge, his wiry thews tensed.

The hiss of vapour drew near.

Its stench stung his nostrils.

He held his breath.

The cloud rounded the corner, bearing guards and a howling wizard.

Kyembe sprang.

Like a leopard, he pounced on Djehuti, seizing him from between his surprised warriors. He caught the wizard's horn in one hand and seized his throat with the other, bearing down with iron strength.

They toppled from the cloud. Djehuti gasped out a choked cry, his eyes wild as the wind whipped past them. The Sengezian braced himself, guiding the wizard between him and the steep, jagged slope as it came up to meet them.

With a bone-shaking crash, Djehuti's body shattered and slid headfirst down the incline—spraying loose rock—with Kyembe atop him, using his corpse as a sled. The white veil wicked red as the body shredded like old cloth. Streaks of crimson painted the mountainside. With a growl, the Spirit Killer aimed the wizard's broken form, launching it from the slope straight for the river.

Above, the sorcerous cloud faded; shrieking guards dropped.

The river writhed below.

They crashed through its surface.

Breath left the Sengezian's body. The River of Scales pulled him and the ruin of Djehuti into the churning waves, dragging them down like ragdolls. The wizard's dead eyes bore into the Sengezian's as if mocking him. With a desperate kick to Djehuti's chest, Kyembe pushed upward, clutching the object of power. One final kick saw his face break the surface, his mouth gulping air.

The world swam and a weak laugh escaped his lips. He sank into blackness.

When he awoke, he was mummified.

Or rather, he was bandaged with poultices soaking his wounds, itching badly and stinking worse.

Something rustled, tickling his side.

He cracked an eye to find a boy kneeling beside him on the floor, changing his dressings.

"Child," he croaked in surprise. "What fortune is this? Where am—"

The boy dropped a bandage, fleeing the chamber into the light of the morning sun. "Demon

eyes!" he screamed.

"No. Not again," Kyembe groaned, but the child had already bolted through a bright linen curtain hanging in the doorway. His fading screams slammed into the Sengezians's skull, drawing a groan.

So much for that.

He glanced about.

There was no sign of Djehuti's horn, but his ring was near and his sword lay propped against a sandstone wall inscribed with painted hieroglyphs surrounding three figures etched into it. The first was a woman who bore a scorpion's tail, and she cupped the eastern wind in hand: the goddess Zerlquet. The second was her husband, the crocodile-headed god Soukbi, who bore the western wind.

Above them a great cobra rose, its hood spread, revealing a golden orb that was the sun. This creature was the Sun-Serpent Ashra, lord of the deities of the Nubtukan Empire.

It seemed he was somehow in Nubtuka.

And at the mercy of their wizard-priests?

Kyembe groaned again, pushing himself up.

The curtain parted.

Three figures filled the doorway; two guards in bronze helms flanking a woman in a brilliant white dress.

"Remain here." The woman let the curtain fall, leaving her alone with the Sengezian.

Djehuti's object of power lay in her grip, and her dark eyes watched Kyembe. The lines of living were beginning to mark her face, but hers was a beauty that had distilled like powerful spirits.

Her eyes were of perfect symmetry, from the galena swirling at their corners to the malachite dying her lids an emerald hue. A jewelled tiara caught her midnight bob, framing the light brown of her cheeks. She moved with the regal precision of a general, and Kyembe knew at once she was dangerous.

"Thank your luck, stranger," her voice was smooth as date wine. "A temple servant was fishing and came upon you floating in the River of Scales: undrowned and unspoiled by crocodiles."

Kyembe watched her closely. "Luck would have seen me not in the river at all. Instead, I gladly thank both servant… and you. Where do I find myself? And why have you saved me?"

"You are in the temple of Zerlquet. Are you familiar with her?"

"Your empire's goddess of wind, medicine, fertility, and death."

"You know her ways… good. I am her servant." She poured herself into a chair against the wall. Her long, curved fingernails followed the horn's hieroglyphs. "And I would be a poor servant if I denied medicine to one in need."

"I…" Kyembe paused, "do not recall the goddess' kindness extending to half-drowned strangers."

The priestess' eyes were tracing the lines of his body, then fell upon his ring. It shone in the low light, bearing the unearthly face of a beautiful, horned woman within the parted teeth of a skull. "A strange bit of jewelry. Your object of power, I presume? And this," she raised the horn, "belonged to the wizard Djehuti. How came you by it?"

Kyembe measured the distance to his sword. "Were you allies?" he asked.

"I sought to hire him; he should have been in the city two days ago." She looked at the sun-serpent on the wall. "But holy Ashra spread his hood and Soukbi bore the moon through the night twice… and no Djehuti. Then you wash into Zinai holding his object of power in a death-grip."

The Sengezian gave a shrug. "He tried to cheat and kill me. That somewhat offended me, and so it ended poorly for him."

The priestess cursed. "A duck's weight of pearls were harvested from the Sea of Gods for his payment. And now you tell me he is dead?"

Kyembe's eyes came alight with interest. Perhaps his luck should be thanked, after all; he might have his life, but most of his worldly wealth was lost in the mountains.

"He is dead, but this is a good thing for you," he said.

A perfectly sculpted eyebrow rose above her painted eyelid. "How so, stranger?"

He gingerly sat up, spreading his arms. "I am Kyembe of Sengezi; you may not have Djehuti, but you have the man who bested him. Why summon the jackal when the lion is here?"

Now her other brow rose. "Kyembe? The one they call the Spirit Killer? Ah, red eyes. The pointed ears. I might have known. They say you are a wizard, and that you slay demons."

"They speak truth, then, though I slay many other things."

The ghost of a smile played across her lips. "I am in need of a slayer. Zerlquet plays mysterious games to bring you to me. But a half-dead slayer is of little use."

Kyembe felt the eldritch energies coursing through his being and reached for his ring. She made no move to stop him.

"I have ways to mend myself quickly, now that I am awake." He slid the object of power onto his finger.

"Good." She handed Djehuti's horn to the Spirit Killer. "Do what I need, and you will have the pearls. I will call for a meal for you, then you will join me in the temple's holy chamber."

"Many thanks. Now, what did you need a slayer and wizard for… miss?"

36

"I am Priestess Takhat." Her eyes hardened. "There is murder in my city of Zinai, committed by no mortal. The killer has taken many lives, including my handmaiden's. I want you to end it."

As Takhat set flame to a platter of sacrificial figs, a towering figure glided into her temple's holy chamber.

Kyembe of Sengezi was free of his bandages, and he cut a fine silhouette.

Broad of shoulder, yet lean as a blade, he moved like water. Wiry thews corded his form, and large eyes peered from a face like that of a handsome woman.

She gave a soft sigh.

"Greetings." He adjusted his sword and strode to her with a smile. "Thank you for the food and for saving my life, of course. Where am I to begin?"

She chuckled. "First, we go to my husband's temple."

"Husband?" His face grew stricken. "By the stars, a boon for him, but a loss for me and many men in the world, and some women as well."

She paused in surprise and... something else.

Well. *This* was a bit of a thrill.

"That wagging tongue will land you in trouble, Spirit Killer."

"It has, and yet I live and it wags still." His smile deepened.

"There is time yet for it to catch up with you." Takhat turned to her new handmaiden polishing the ancient statue of First Priestess Tiye.

"Anipe," she called.

The young woman startled. "Yes, Priestess Takhat?"

"Watch the sacrificial fires, and when the sun reaches the feet of Tiye," she pointed to a beam of radiance pouring through one of the skylights, "you may open the temple."

"Y-yes, priestess, but the crowd outside is ugly." Anipe bowed so low, she threatened to topple. "What would you have me do?"

Takhat's lip twitched.

By Zerlquet, did she miss Bunefer. Her late handmaiden was clever and held the dangerous ambition of an asp: a woman after Takhat's own heart.

Her loss was a deep wound, in many ways.

"If the crowd looks dangerous, only open the side gate to women who are with child: the mob will be reluctant to push them aside. At least for now."

"I will do as you ask!" Anipe cried in relief.

"Mmm, see that you do."

Garbed in cloaks long bleached by desert sun, Kyembe and Takhat emerged from a tunnel and slipped into the sun-blasted streets of Zinai. Pulling his hood higher, Kyembe spied a crowd swarming the temple's outer walls, hurling demands and pleas.

Tension hung in the air, the sort that a single spark could ignite.

"A grim congregation." He strode with his hand near his blade. "Did Zerlquet withhold her favour, allowing plague to run through your city?"

"It is not Zerlquet alone who faces their wrath." She pulled her hood higher. "They gather in front of all temples in Zinai—day and night—crying out for the return of their sons and daughters from Mabatia and an end to these killings."

"Well, I cannot blame them, but I see now why a sack of pearls awaits me." Kyembe watched the inconsolable crowds, all grief and rage, as he and the priestess passed into wider boulevards of hot sandstone.

She wiped her brow with a kerchief. "Would that we could have taken the palanquin. The heat is murderous today, and... ah."

She spied the temple of Soukbi from a street corner.

A mob half a hundred strong gathered before its outer gate, jeering and shouting.

"Ah, do something, Buneb," Takhat whispered darkly.

"Your husband?" Kyembe noted steam rising from the temple's skylights.

"He is high wizard-priest of Soukbi, god in favour in Zinai. A powerful man, but... well, come, we will take a hidden passage to the temple's holy chamber."

Steam choked the holy chamber of Soukbi, stifling the breath with a lethargy that stole one's strength. From somewhere within the haze, the hiss of water in copper basins came, boiled by vents channeling heat from deep within the earth. Hazy silhouettes stood in the fog, and only the twitch of life and the odour of scented oils separated acolytes from carven statues.

Strange currents of sorcery struck Kyembe's senses as he and the still perspiring Takhat slipped from the passage and made their way toward the looming form of Soukbi's statue.

At its feet, a shape materialized from the haze; a man lounged upon a divan, heavyset and so still, he seemed dead. Grey eyes numbed by listlessness bore the countenance of late middle age. Filth stained his robe.

The sight struck the Sengezian, stilling him for a heartbeat. Those eyes... that numbness. He had seen them before. A memory returned: a younger man with a shining ring, sitting by the burnt body of an old demon.

A man who had filled a hunger for vengeance...

...a man who had lost purpose.

He shook the ancient ghosts from his thoughts and stepped forward.

"Husband," Takhat greeted Buneb.

"Wife." Buneb's tone was feeble.

"Priestess," a sharp voice spoke, one belonging to an acolyte who stepped to Buneb's side, his eyes filled with vigour. Oil slicked a fine, black beard.

Takhat hardly spared him a glance and he bristled.

But Kyembe paid him even less mind, his eyes were watching the ceiling.

Something had caused the hairs on the back of his neck to rise. Sorcerous currents... and disquiet at the way the steam swirled.

It reminded the Sengezian of the vapours spewed from Djehuti's horn.

He brought his hand to his sword, barely listening as Takhat introduced him.

"Kyembe of Sengezi will serve me in destroying the evil that plagues us, Buneb." Takhat watched her husband. "Have you... taken your own measures? The other temples follow your example."

"This is a passing storm." Buneb toyed with a carven crocodile's tooth hanging from his neck. "The sand will drink the water in time."

Takhat stiffened. "Buneb, I cannot calm the people much longer. What happened to the man who—"

"This is not your temple, Priestess Takhat," the acolyte's voice cracked through the steam. "And it is Soukbi who is most favoured in Zinai, not Zerlquet. You will have respect."

"Soukbi might not be most favoured much longer, Iuty." Takhat fixed him with a glare. "How long until the mobs cast down every temple wall as they did in Faiyar when our forces fell against the Medjan? Buneb must cast away this bleakness and act!"

"Act? As you have?" Iuty's smile was a hyena's. "This wanderer you have hired, what is he, the fourth? There was that woman, the Bronze Spider? Found dead before your temple.

Then the Terror of Merza. Also found dead before your temple. Then the wizard you promised would be our salvation, he did not even reach the walls of the city! And now..."

The acolyte threw a nasty sneer at Kyembe. "Begone, stranger, unless you too desire a cold bed before the Temple of Zerlquet."

Kyembe pulled his eyes away from the rising steam. "Were you speaking to me?"

Iuty paused. "Er, yes."

"What was it you said? I was occupied."

"You—"

"Do not worry yourself Iuty," Buneb said in torpid tones. "Ashra will open his hood and welcome days long after Zinai is dust. Nothing matters."

"Buneb—" Takhat started.

"Go back to your temple, wife. What will be, will be."

Takhat said not another word, striding back to the passage.

Kyembe watched the steam for a few heartbeats, then nodded to Buneb. "May you choose purpose once more. Or may peace choose you."

Then he followed the priestess.

The pair did not speak until they were deep in the tunnel.

"He was not always like this." Takhat's voice held a defensive note. "Buneb the Young they called him; he drove demons from the temple of Soukbi, only allowing those that served his god to remain. He was wonderful... Now that wasp, Iuty, stands ready to usurp. You must act quickly. There are caves beneath Zinai, where Hori went to search for Bunefer. You might start there."

"I do not think so." Kyembe cocked his head, measuring how far sound travelled the tunnel's length. "I have already found your problem."

Takhat startled. "What?"

His voice dropped low.

"Something hides within that steam, high above our heads. Something not of this world."

The priestess bristled. "In the temple's holy chamber?"

"Indeed. I intend to return tonight; is there another hidden passage? One that I might watch from unseen?"

Her lips took a vicious twist, half-smile and half-snarl. "Iuty... perhaps he stole Buneb's object of power to work his deviltry. Yes, there is a place where we can observe the chamber in secret."

"Good. Tonight, I shall—wait, *we*?"

"*We*." Takhat's eyes flared. "I would not miss this for all the water in Zinai."

The priestess and Sengezian crept through another passage to a small door beside Soukbi's statue. Kyembe opened it a mere crack so they might remain unnoticed.

"What are we looking for?" Takhat peered into the moonlight.

"You will know soon." The Sengezian's crimson eyes slid over the dancing steam.

For a time, there was nothing.

And then—

"Someone comes," Kyembe whispered.

Furtive footsteps slipped through the holy chamber.

A wicked smile curled Takhat's lips. Iuty, no doubt! The ambitious acolyte had overplayed his hand. Now he would... would...

What was this?

That sly gait conjured a recollection from some twenty years ago.

Those steps would glide through the night; a subtle promise of delight slipping through the family courtyard and toward Takhat's bedchamber window... which she would always leave open.

Young days. Bright days.

But the man who once made

those steps had long faded from her life, taken by a grey listlessness.

Until now.

Her husband Buneb emerged from the steam and into the centre of the holy chamber.

She gasped.

A hideous vigour filled his eyes.

A smile—he actually smiled—as he raised the carven crocodile's tooth; his object of power. Words boiled from his lips, so sharp and foul they pierced the ear.

She cupped her mouth in horror. A tongue of demons.

The wizard-priests could conjure such creatures to serve their deity, but to do so in the holy chamber was blasphemy! What was this madness?

"Look," Kyembe whispered, nodding toward the ceiling.

Takhat watched, transfixed, as a strange coalescence oozed from on high and descended, hovering before Buneb. Something swam through the mist—she could swear there were faces boiling within—and an evil intellect chilled the air, setting her primal instincts screaming.

"New thrills await, my hound." Buneb passed his hand through the creature fondly. "And those who displease me abound. Hunt for me. Bring me to life again."

Betrayal cut Takhat like a cursed blade.

This could not be! All the deaths in Zinai all these months and... Bunefer. He knew how much she meant to her, and *he* was the one who had killed her?

All remaining love for this man she thought she knew withered within, like a desert bloom beneath the merciless sun.

Rage cauterised her inner wounds, but sense cooled them.

She could not—

A glint beside her; the Segenzian's sword slid free.

She caught his wrist. Those crimson eyes turned to her as she shook her head.

A puzzled look, but the sword slid back into his belt.

Takhat reached out and eased the door closed.

The sliver of light from Buneb's chamber was abruptly replaced by darkness. "We must go," she hissed.

Kyembe watched her through the dark.

A slight scrape sent a bloom of fright through Buneb, and he whirled on the secret passage. Yet his ragged breaths soon calmed when he gazed upon his beautiful demon, and he drew courage from it. "We are blessed tonight. Someone spying? How delightful, prey presents itself! Shall we follow, my pet? Shall we see who it is? Perhaps *Takhat's* new hound."

He grinned at the thing hidden in mist, his heartbeat quickening.

How long had it been since *anything* quickened his heart?

"A hound she might have, but your fangs are sharper. I should have summoned you years ago."

"This is an abomination." Takhat paced before the statue of her goddess.

Her eyes bled rage, though not a tear stained her galena. Much like the holy chamber of Soukbi's temple, Zerlquet's was empty at night, leaving only Kyembe and the priestess in the moonlight.

"What would you have me do?" Kyembe thumbed his sword's pommel. "I could slay him—"

"No!" She whirled on him. "He is... my husband." She spat the word as though it were bile. "If he were to fall, I stand to replace him as the favoured priest in this city. But, Iuty would throw suspicion at my feet and turn the other temples against me."

She looked into Kyembe's eyes, taking a step toward him.

"No... this must be resolved, but..."

"My condolences," he sighed. "Betrayal stabs more surely than any knife, be it bronze or," he glanced at his sword, "sky iron."

"Yes. And now I must use wit, not bronze. You... your part in this is done. You will have the pearls for your silence."

"Mm... if you wish me not to kill Buneb, that is your choice. But the demon? Its very presence offends me, so I will destroy it. Its conjurer will be left to you."

She gave him an appraising look. "Does that have to be right away?" Her eyes slid over his form. "Kyembe, did you mean what you said? About my marriage being a loss for you? It seems that it is a loss for me as well. And I do not like to lose."

She took another step forward, he could feel her heat.

Her curved nails bit into his tunic.

His eyes danced as his arms wrapped around her. "Truly? Before the gaze of your goddess?"

Takhat was pulling him to her parting lips. "She is a goddess of fertility and medicine." The priestess breathed. "And *this* is medicine; I would be a poor servant to deny it."

Lips pressed to lips in the moonlight.

Wrath transfixed Buneb in the mist-filled tunnel.

The sounds had reached him through the temple of Zerlquet's secret passage, burning his ears from her betrayal. Rage choked him so thoroughly, he could not move from within the demon-mist.

His wife? How dare she!

"Betrayal will be met with death," he snarled. "Come!"

The mist billowed, surging forward by its master's command, eager to slay.

An evil hiss halted Kyembe as he buckled his belt.

His hand fell on his sword hilt and his eyes shot to Takhat; the priestess had dressed and was humming as she straightened her jewellery.

"You should go." His body tensed like a leopard's.

"What? Something—" She turned, following his gaze.

"The demon." His blade blurred into his hand, its sky iron shining in the moonlight. His ring gleamed and Djehuti's object of power bounced on his belt.

Takhat gasped.

A hidden passage opened in the wall. Buneb emerged in a cloak of mist, his eyes cracked by lines of blood, and his lips pulled back in a snarl.

Demonic faces shimmered around him.

"Dog!" he hissed at Kyembe. "My demon will tear out your insides—"

The Spirit Killer wordlessly lifted his ring, calling upon his eldritch energies.

A sound thrummed the air, like a great breath being drawn. The ring upon his finger flared so brightly, it stung the eye. The Sengezian grimaced as the magic sent terrible burns coiling up his arm.

Buneb squealed like a frightened pig, scrambling back and frantically pulling the door shut behind him.

With a crackle like bursting bone, a beam of white hellfire seared through the air, blasting near the thick door. Sandstone flared with the orange incandescence of molten stone, forming a vast chasm in the rock.

Through it, Kyembe saw Buneb in flight.

But his demon-mist still surged forward.

"Go!" the Sengezian cried to Takhat.

The priestess gave him a look and fled, slamming the chamber doors behind her.

Now it was Kyembe and the mist in a sealed chamber, stalking each other through moonlight.

Twisted faces roiled in the fog, long tongues flicked out, splitting in two. He snarled; hellfire had not harmed Buneb's demon, and his sword would be useless against mist.

He darted toward its flank like flowing water, but the demon shot at him with a gale's speed. Cursing, Kyembe leapt back, the mist in pursuit as he retreated across the chamber.

It flowed past columns and over statues, closing the distance.

How could he kill air?

He could not cut it. He could not burn—

Djehuti's horn and the scent of its vapours came back to him: like brimstone and oil. Both would set the air aflame. His burnt hand ripped the horn from his belt as he threw his eldritch energies into it. Terrible magics crashed through his body, bursting blood vessels as he spat words of power.

Agony tore at his mind, but he hardened his will and vapours—like a tempest—swirled from the horn's tip.

With a roar, Kyembe cast it through the mist to the room's centre. The creature did not pause; faces mocked him, as though they had not a care in the world.

Claws and fangs of mist coalesced, scraping along stone as the demon pursued.

I will eat you from the inside, little mortal, its voice was a corrupt whisper that stung the mind.

Kyembe snarled—blood trickling from his lips, head throbbing like a titan's drum—but he raced through the chamber, buying time while those sorcerous vapours saturated the air. He held his breath as the odour seared his nostrils; vapours stung his eyes and burnt his skin. His lungs screamed for air, but a single breath could mean his end.

Green smoke grew so thick, the mist slowed, suffused in it.

Kyembe was ready.

He sprinted from the mist-demon, leaping onto the statue of Priestess Tiye and catapulted to the nearest pillar, his sword thrusting. The point bit and held as he scaled the rock, his eyes turned toward the skylight. Another spring and he caught the edge, pulling himself up into the moonlight.

He channelled his eldritch energies.

His ring flared, aimed at the vapour-filled chamber below.

The demon mist rose hungrily like a starving cobra, its mouths rolling with mirth as green smoke infused its form.

"Laugh at this," the Spirit Killer said. "Let us see who burns who from the inside, little demon."

Hellfire shot out in a blinding beam, striking the vapours.

An explosion through the holy chamber.

The force of the blast knocked Kyembe back as laughter became screams. Every speck of living fog burned. Buneb's hound writhed, solidifying, clawing at nothingness.

The flames licked at Djehuti's horn.

A thunder clap. Stone cracked. The temple shook.

The demon shrieked like the very wind was screaming; terrified cries erupted from the crowd outside even as Buneb's pet faded into a wisp of smoke and vanished.

Taking a long breath of fresh desert air, Kyembe of Sengezi savoured the beating of his own heart.

By the stars, he lived but...

Buneb had sought to kill him. That... somewhat offended him.

The high priest slid back into the steam of Soukbi's holy chamber, a hacking cough shuddering through his chest. He had returned to the tunnel door in

Zerlquet's temple once the stranger was distracted—watching through the hole Takhat's new pet had melted in the rock, but then those foul vapours filled the room.

A mere half-breath had nearly killed him.

Worse, he had emerged from the tunnel near the crowd before the temple. He might have been seen.

And now, his demon was gone.

He shuddered at those dark thoughts. What would he do without his servant, his only joy? He would never again live in greyness.

Perhaps call another demon.

He began—

A hand fell on his shoulder, spinning him about with iron strength.

"What was that you said? You would have your demon tear out my insides?" A deep voice sent a wave of fear through Buneb. All traces of grey spirits fled. "Let us see what yours look like."

Crimson eyes blazed through the steam. A blade flashed.

"You chose the wrong purpose."

"**M**urdered?" Takhat gasped.

"Gutted and hung like a pig!" Iuty snarled in the moonlight. "Is this your doing?"

The priestess' jaw hardened. "You have it backwards. My husband tried to kill *me*."

"Accusations, but no witnesses," the acolyte growled.

"His demon's shriek could have woken the dead, and some in the crowd outside saw a man fleeing: one who was Buneb's image."

"You dishonour your late husband with such words," Iuty spewed.

"He dishonoured me when he sent a demon into my temple. He dishonoured Soukbi when he summoned it in his holy chamber."

"Lies. When I rise to power—"

"You will not," Takhat pronounced. "What do you think will happen when word spreads of *who* caused the murders? Soukbi will not be most favoured in Zinai any longer, and Iuty will need to learn politeness. As is *befitting* an acolyte."

Iuty sputtered, whirling and storming from her chambers.

Takhat let out a sigh, reaching for a mug of beer. She felt more tired than she had in months.

She raised the mug to drink when light knocking drew her gaze to the window.

"By Zerlquet!" she hissed.

Kyembe stood in the moonlight, his hands dripping and crimson eyes flashing. "Greetings, priestess."

She looked at his hands. "Is that... what I fear it is?"

"It is water." He approached her, stopping very close. "I washed before coming here; I am no barbarian. You have heard, then?"

"I have. Why?"

"He tried to kill me... and once he did, what was merely your affair became mine."

"...unreasonable, but understandable," she sighed, her mind racing.

If it came out—and it would—that Takhat's hired man had slain Buneb, then Iuty could turn things to his favour, and by the time it became clear that her dead husband had caused these horrors, it would be too late for her.

Iuty would act quickly.

So she would need to act quicker.

A stab of guilt went through her breast...

...but what could she do?

Takhat placed a palm against Kyembe's cheek and looked into those crimson eyes. She never did ask why they were such an inhuman hue. Now, she likely never could. "What is done is done. You did what you had to... as *all* must.

Where will you go from here?"

Eyes the colour of sweet wine searched hers. Understanding passed between them. "I am not sure yet... perhaps we will meet again, and I can tell you the tale of my next adventure."

"Mmm, perhaps," she said. "Be safe, Spirit Killer. Be well, and may Zerlquet's wind blow you swiftly ahead of all enemies."

"Or may they learn to run from me." He kissed her hand.

Not trusting herself to say any more, Takhat left the room, feeling his eyes on her back. She would inform the temple guard of how it looked like a certain wanderer had turned on her husband. But she would be slow in the telling.

To give him a headstart.

Yet in the whirlwind of dark revelations and her husband's death, she could not shake the feeling she had forgotten something.

Kyembe was already sliding from the window when Takhat closed the door.

He was sure the city guard would be looking for him before the cockerel crowed.

But that was of little importance.

He would make for the river; it would be fitting, as the River of Scales had brought him, so it would carry him away. He would stowaway on a boat headed north and only come out when it reached Mem-Tephi... or perhaps beyond the empire's borders.

Perhaps the City of Zabyalla on the Sea of Gods.

As he darted through the shadows, a horrible realization suddenly struck him.

"By the stars, the pearls!" He scowled. "I did not get paid!"

ABOUT THE AUTHOR

J.M. Clarke is a fantasy writer and social worker located in southeastern Canada, focusing on short stories, novels and web serials in a variety of subgenres, including Dark Fantasy, Epic Fantasy, Progression Fantasy and Sword & Sorcery.

His Sword & Sorcery tales include "The Vapours of Zinai," appearing in *New Edge #0*, "The Curse of Wine," appearing in *A Book of Blades*, as well as *The Dreaming Sceptre*, currently serialized online and due to be published to Amazon.

His debut epic progression fantasy series—*The Mark of the Fool*, published by Aethon Books—will be available for sale through Amazon on September 20th, 2022.

The Grief-Note of Vultures

by Bryn Hammond

Wild donkey has twelve lives at least and gives a legendary meat: strangely fragrant for such a smelly beast, sweet and crumbly as if he's a cross with baklava. Angaj-Duzmut hadn't had a chance at one before—not while on her own. She'd contrived a stalk, which took most of the day, but without an archer as canny as Yoshet in wait, she'd still have lost the kill. The two of them came back triumphant with a dead wild donkey slung between the humps of a camel.

A couple of hours later, Angaj-Duzmut declared, "I haven't eaten better. Even fattened goat in the tents of my people."

Yoshet said, "Nor I, even in the streets of Qocho where every people's food is out to sample."

"I never bit into the equal of this crisp haunch," said Qip with a slap to the remains of its rump, "though I have sat to a queen's feast on the high steppe."

The trader himself had turned the roast on the spit, anointed with orange peel and walnut oil from his stash. He joined in. "My dream dish is my wife's lamb, seethed in milk with cinnamon stick. But wild donkey on the hillside, where a donkey never sighted the likes of me before: he'll live again in my sleep."

Qip, who had four wives, opened wide a wrestler's arm. "Let mine cook for you when our travel together's over. Our circle here, before we go our ways."

They might have been drunk on the donkey. So this is the comradeship of the road, thought Angaj-Duzmut. Temporary—not to be mistaken for guest-friendship in the tents, where to eat with a stranger at your hearth creates a tie for life. Two out of eight at the campfire, Qip and Yoshet, she imagined she might see again once the three-month job was done.

After the roast was laid waste and people lazed, Angaj-Duzmut got up to gather the bones.

"Seriously, we have to clean the site before we sleep?" Lhazo complained.

They were used to her rules around a clean campsite. The townspeople among them teased her for a frugal nomad, but they followed her instructions. A few of them Angaj-Duzmut had to teach to live off-road. This wasn't a convoy serviced by traveler's rests, food stalls on wheels by the roadside, hawkers of wood for your fire. She wouldn't let them strip the woody bushes, either. Growth was rare enough along their ways, and what did they think the wild donkeys ate? Instead, they learned to be self-sufficient: collect dung left by the yaks who pulled their wagons and the camels they rode, dry the pats on baggage felts for use as fuel.

"It isn't that," she told Lhazo. "I need to wrap the bones."

They recognized the phrase. "It's a tribal thing," they explained to each other. "A Qiang custom." Two or three even began to hand her bones they reached from where they sat. She hadn't interrupted the feast by stopping them tossing bones on the ground.

"You wrap the bones in a piece of the hide, and the animal comes alive again from them—isn't that it? Do you, um, do you believe a new animal grows from the bones, or is it more a symbol of replenishment?"

"What I believe doesn't matter." In the Black Tents, Angaj-Duzmut hadn't been known for observance—quite the contrary. But she cared about respect towards the wild donkey they had eaten. "It's in the attitude."

With the bones wrapped in hide she walked out of the firelight, up the hillside. Her eyes cleared to the night. High on the slope, she stowed the donkey remains by a tussock, crouched there for a while, and listened at a distance to the crew around the fire.

Were a guide's wages worth the hassle of being with other people, settled folk at that? Contempt for a nomad ran strong, even in the type who hired out as van guards. This lot weren't too bad, but she found herself exhausted.

At least they were trustworthy, or if they weren't she'd have herself to blame. As the expedition's guide she'd had a voice in the hire of guards—since she answered to the bandits for their conduct. Now she knew the life, perhaps in future she'd sign on as a hand with vans that went through government stations— if the city god of Fattimbet got over his feud with her. Until the god forgot her, documented travel wasn't possible, and she'd sought a trader with similar requirements: no inspections. A single trader, light with high-profit merchandise, whom a goatherd from the mountains might lead by desolate ways—around the marshes where a bandits' Commonwealth ruled in lieu of the state. Only a bandits' toll to pay, set at slightly less than the equivalent government fees.

Last year, in escape from the city god of Fattimbet, Angaj-Duzmut had spent a summer with the Scarlet Jackets gang. Its Utszu had a fling with her, and out of that affair she was named a Friend of the Bandits. Such title came with perquisites. Angaj-Duzmut wore a badge, reeds neatly twisted with pressed blossoms to signify the Utszu's famous spear, Pear in Flower. The trader's van she led flew a scarlet flag. Huge in area, the bandits' Commonwealth held an estimated population of three Fattimbets or the capital city Irighaya. Without safe-conduct no trader would take his valuables near it. To fake safe-conduct? That got you strung up on the outskirts of the marshes, in grisly imitation of the government's exhibits of dead criminals at town gates. But a bandit's word was scripture. Whether or not the Utszu kept their fling ongoing, Angaj-Duzmut rode around the marshes in perfect confidence of safety.

What bothered her, then? Angaj-Duzmut liked a simple life where she only had to look out for herself. On the other hand, she did enjoy the hearty eating every night, and at the end of this job she'd come away with funds to eat in future.

Still in high spirits next day, they started up journey songs. Except Qip, who refused to sing her part. Qip came from the taiga—forests far north above the Great Steppe. They classed her as tribal too. "In the taiga, singing is how spirits talk. People do not sing out in the open, for fear we call them to us unaware."

Almost everywhere else, journey songs were requisite— so they told her, and Qip shook her blunt head in a mild way that didn't spoil the mood.

Singing soon had another damper. That day they climbed off the salty flats around the great marshes of the bandits to cross a low spine of mountains. Angaj-Duzmut was more familiar with the north side of these mountains, which were higher, almost contiguous with steppe. In contrast to either side, grass steppe or salty hollows, these hills were an oasis, watered by a rain unknown beneath. The yaks tugged with new vigour. The camels, onto whose feet they had sewn

leather slips against the cutting salt, now slid on the wet ground and groaned in the perpetual rain.

Angaj-Duzmut hated the wet too, battling in goat's-hair trousers that became a sodden mat. Her home mountains, a month east, never saw a lick of water, and better for it. At least they kept the dung dry in its sacks.

On the south side of the range grew rhubarb—bigger than Angaj-Duzmut had known rhubarb to grow. Stalks to twelve feet high thrust out of sprawling nests of leaves, each leaf up to five feet across. Rhubarb root, said the trader, was a commodity he might have dug up in the spring. Once flowered, the root coarsened and nobody bought. Shaved and steeped in tea, its medicine cured stomach ailments and quenched fever. "But this stuff's far too monstrous." He batted aside a ragged elephant's ear of a leaf.

The crimson flower clusters and purpled leaves threw Angaj-Duzmut back to the summer before. She drifted away from the annoying noise of rain into a memory of the Scarlet Jackets' Utszu in mock-combat with a tall rhubarb flower stalk in place of her spear. A leaping spear dance, a thrusting flower spike instead of blade, and the Utszu laughing— then collapsing by the side of Duzmut, stripping off her scarlet jacket in the sun, her arms damp and pungent and eye-tauntingly exercised.

Angaj-Duzmut's daydream about the Utszu's arms was interrupted when Lhazo shoved her shoulder for attention and yelled in her ear. The rain, slapping on the rhubarb thickets, made a racket.

"Pit stop." Lhazo pointed. "Temple gruel, but underneath a roof."

Up ahead, rooves of mustard-yellow tiles, a glimpse of

turquoise-painted walls within a grove of juniper. A religious house on the wild mountainside remote even from a road to any town. Contemplatives creep in where soldiers fear to tread.

"I'm afraid not," Angaj-Duzmut answered in a shout. "You can't trust a temple not to have state ties."

"This close to the Commonwealth?"

"I don't like its location." In Angaj-Duzmut's home mountains, the nearest government station stayed discretely distant, while temples intruded right among the tents and attempted to convert children in their schools. "The Commonwealth is a state within the state, and the Utszu on the throne"—for the gangs took that title in mockery of the king—"knows he can't send his army in without humiliation and military disaster in the marshes. But a temple of lamas withdrawn from the world can keep watch on his behalf."

The trader had come across to listen. He weighed in on Angaj-Duzmut's side. "I might want to use this route again, and I'm certain our guide needs to keep her secrets. Let's not tip off the authorities by temple-visiting."

So they angled away from the temple. After half an hour they had a view of it on a level and saw it was abandoned anyway. A gnarled arm of juniper was in process of twisting one roof off like a lid. Of its nine rooves— holy number—three were intact. Yet the turquoise walls weren't weathered, gaudy against a pink sea of rhubarb.

"The bandits must have rid themselves of their neighbour," guessed Uneet. "Only a winter or two ago, by the pretty brick."

The prospect of the temple was an excuse to rest from the effort of tugging sulky camels—for they didn't try to ride in the wet. They too were in juniper trees now. Angaj-Duzmut had found a seat under an umbrella of scabby boughs when above them, the juniper exploded.

Birds—giant birds the size of the camels—thrashed through the thickly prickled trees and stretched their feet towards the people underneath. Three-toed feet with talons sheathed in the wrinkled skin of vultures. Beaks that belonged to the vulture species local to the mountains, but these birds were bizarre. The one busy trashing Duzmut's tree to get at her wore on its flat head an eyeball, a naked human eyeball football-sized, sprouting on its stalk like a mushroom. Another, crashing into branches that sheltered Qip and Yoshet, had growing from its belly a hanging human arm, whose huge hand clumsily snatched in a fist between the snatching feet. A third had thumped to ground and waddled in with outthrust neck and that awkward vulture's gait, the more ungainly because it dragged along with it spools of veiny skin—the smooth, nude strips you see when they cut and peel skin from convicts in the town square. Uneet, its target, wriggled beneath a wagon and hugged the axle.

Duzmut had witnessed scenes of vultures mobbing intruders at their feast—including human intruders. Her group had stumbled onto a feast ground and upset the birds, only these were birds with human body parts and bigger than the rhubarb round about.

They were demolishing the juniper, even Duzmut's vast old tree, a thick wicker shield against the rain. Tree bits littered down so that Duzmut had to protect her eyes. She opened them to the sight of three vultures in the air, and between them, suspended on their hooks, Balastu.

Balastu was heavyset: they joked that he made his camel creak. Now vultures jostled for him the way riders in a buzqash game tussle for a goatskin stuffed with sand. He swung from one grip to another with the passivity of the goatskin sack. Unlike in buzqash, the birds seemed only to mock-compete—Duzmut saw it was a game to them. They squeezed their talons daintily to keep him kicking. Yet vultures' feet the size of horses' heads have to prick a vital fairly soon. When Balastu went entirely limp, they threw him away.

The others didn't stop to watch and waste the vultures' inattention. Lhazo bellowed, "Make for the temple," and tried to heave two yoked yaks in that direction. Uneet rolled out from under the wagon before wheels or yak hooves turned on him. The trader went to Lhazo's assistance, swung astride a panicky yak to coax it forward. It and its yoke-mate plunged into the dip between them and the temple. Everybody in the open, whatever else they did, whirled their swords above their heads or randomly stabbed upwards at the air.

Lhazo had lived in the capital Irighaya, the trader based in Qocho city. Their instinct was to run towards a wall. Perhaps they expected sanctuary in holy precincts, abandoned or not. Whereas Angaj-Duzmut, a nomad from the Black Tents, never saw a wall she liked the look of, and if she had a faith, it was the Black Faith, without priest or book or doctrine, that predated the Temples of the Wise.

It was difficult to argue in the bawl of camels, the giant birds' attack, and the rain. Angaj-Duzmut settled for going rearguard, to at least keep them together and the animals intact. Qip had the sense to throw her coat over her camel's head and had much less trouble wrestling him. The others caught on to this trick.

They clashed iron blade on blade overhead, they *yahhed* the birds away as if from a battle site or butchery. Lhazo sliced off a sheet of human skin from the bird tangled round with peel from the flayers. The piece dropped, perversely, right on Lhazo's head and slimed around his throat as if alive. He squawked, threw down his sword to use both hands and cast the snake of skin as far from him as possible.

Yoshet sent home an arrow into the flesh of the human arm that dangled under the belly of his bird. The arrow fixed, to cause yet more inconvenience to a flying vulture. But its screech was such that he too fumbled his wrist through his bow to free his hands and clap them on his ears. It was a screech half-bird, half-human, as loud as a camel's worst straight in your earhole, and somehow resonant, down to the pit of your stomach and at the same time up, up from a residual sense people have of the past, even when they did not live it. There is a common memory, an omniscience of souls in between lives on earth.

It was a spirit's call.

The third bird, the eyeball-bird, buzzed Duzmut in the rear. She chose to meet it eye to eye. She did not swipe her sword, and the bird didn't seize her with its feet. They stared at one another. The eye seemed half-aware—not alert and fierce like the vulture's eyes but dazed, off in its own dream of consciousness. Similarly, on the arm-bird the human hand moved more slowly than the bird-feet—in imitation of their grasp but with a delay. These were no dead appendages—they had an independence, although merged with the birds. As Duzmut stared she came to feel a nightmare suffocation, a sense of no escape, as if her existence boiled down to one moment thick as stew left on the fire to scorch and catch, yet she knew she must despair to ever boil away. Emotions spill out of spirits, puddles you can step into by accident. Duzmut stopped ogling the eyeball.

The temple had a wide court-yard, space for vehicles, amenities for pilgrims. They pushed their camels into stone stalls under shelter, jammed the yaks' faces to a wall and tied them tightly by the nose. Luckily the trader had a relationship with his yaks, animals he had reared. They seemed to think the end-days weren't upon them while he spoke to them calmly.

The great vultures flapped outside the gates. Either averse to enter, or else they had them trapped. In tiers jutted the nine yellow-tiled rooves with gilt-written scriptures on the eaves. The gates, too, were crisscrossed with letters. Spells to keep them out, unless, like an unlettered goatherd who spent her child-hood skipping temple-school, the vultures thought writing meant bad news.

Most of the group found refuge in the main hall, where a stalk of rhubarb had seeded itself in front of a saint's statue on a plinth and shot up to tickle its chin. Angaj-Duzmut, reluctant to go in, noticed another access to the courtyard. A path led upwards to a grotto in a cliff-face. Often temples were sited beside caves of sacred art to host those who came to worship at the images. By its ornamental archway and mosaic path, by the way the nine rooves tilted to it like hats in obeisance, the grotto was the focus of the temple. And through the ping and splatter of rain on tiles Angaj-Duzmut's ear caught from up the path a wailing—a particular wailing she had heard before. Once she had killed a griffon vulture in the mountains and gone to sleep that night. Her sleep had been pierced by a sound of lamentation she mistook for human, and she went out to search, but the cry led her back to her dead griffon where its mate stood by the body and gave voice. Griffon vultures almost never vocalize—only a rare wail in grief.

A memory of that cry came from the grotto.

Angaj-Duzmut poked her head into the hall and told the others, "There are holy caves, and I suspect the trouble is in them. I'm going to explore."

Lhazo and Uneet had equipped themselves with a brass bell and a silk-wrapped whisk, which they brandished in both hands with conviction. "Is that where the demons broke through? This temple has become a demon lodge, but still they are afraid of sanctity. If we ward ourselves with relics—even a section of holy wood"—two others of them were at work wrecking the shrine for this purpose—"around our beasts and the wagons, they'll

46

leave us alone. They must have besieged the lamas here until they were frightened away."

Angaj-Duzmut didn't think a horsetail whisk, whether for flies or dust or as the Wise say, for afflictions, likely to be effective against whatever these birds were. Except Qip, everybody in her party—however irreligious in daily life—were Followers of the Wise. She hadn't expected religious differences to matter.

"Our birds don't look like demons," she began. Demons frowned from doorjambs on nearly every door in every town. Blue-black or clay-red, the same wherever you went. "You've got to look at the specifics of them." The specificity of these amalgams meant to her they were spirits with a story.

Every spirit has a story.

"I don't want to walk out against them with a fly swat," she continued, "but if the grotto is the origin, we might find out what we need to know."

"Instead, you'd walk into a demons' lair?"

"See, I don't believe in demons as such. Better if only I go."

"What do they have to do, claw out your eyes and eat them? I never saw such obviously cursed things in my life."

This wasn't the time for religious disputation. 'Obviously cursed' was one idea, and 'demons' quite another.

The trader intervened. "Let her try. Native religion sees an infinity of spirits, and they take them as they find them. The attitude is practical. I rather like it. Our guide might have knowledge as pertinent as a scroll-learned cleric."

At least her client hadn't forgotten he answered to a goatherd on this trip. Duzmut didn't wait for more discussion. She crossed her short spear and her sword over her head and stepped onto the path.

The wail drew her. A whistle-wail, flutey, almost sweet—straight from her dreams the night after she killed the griffon vulture's mate.

Advanced along the path, she glanced behind and saw the three giant vultures now perched close together on the main hall's roof. They ignored her, busily clutching tiles. At the mouth of the caves, she saw from above how other rooves had been staved in—by the sheer weight of the vultures or application of their feet. Not a lot of sanctuary, she thought. What if the temple attracted them, what if the holy things were targets? She was certain they had run the wrong way.

Duzmut entered the grotto. Layout conventional for caves of sacred art: frescoes from floor to high ceiling lit by cracks of daylight. But one expected the cracks to spotlight saintly faces. There were no saints here. The figure presiding at the entrance peered down upon Duzmut with the aspect of a stern magistrate and a magistrate's staff of office, except he was a blue-skinned demon and had goat horns.

A goatherd wasn't put off by horns. On the other hand, magistrates weren't a species she was fond of. This portrait, an individual yet somehow essence of magistrate, without the horns and hue might have pointed his sharp nose at her in the justice halls of Fattimbet.

Duzmut pushed past him, onto scenes of hell.

Hell wasn't a popular topic for religious frescoes—audiences liked celestial scenes of bliss and blessedness. These, minutely rendered, were scenes of punishment as though the town square on sentence-day had ramped up to a frenzy, as though blue-skinned executioners and constabulary and clerks had seized half the citizens for correction. For the spectator, the only rest was an intersperse of lesser magistrates in

haughty, serene supervision, their fingers fastidiously hidden in their sleeves.

Duzmut's eye was caught by—an eye, an eye she recognized. Held naked, pink stalk dangling, over a writhing body on a plank. Plucked by a demon whose face resembled a dozen bored officers who in the past had had business with Angaj-Duzmut. Paint peeled around the eye, around the victim and the demon. Despite its deteriorated condition, the anguish of the eyeball leapt out, visceral.

Did the painter possess such uncanny skill that an eyeball almost spoke? Or was the image itself inhabited by spirit, a spirit also entangled with the body of a vulture?

Wandering through the hell scenes, Duzmut found other spots where the paintwork was beginning to peel. Yes, a man being flayed in ribbons from the hips down and watching. A man being lopped at the limbs, his head and neck strained to crane after one of his arms that had lodged under his bench.

All the while, that wail. Within the caves it seemed to come from everywhere. Its grief-note, or else spillover emotion from the unhappy spirits, the haunt-spirits stuck in their moment of trauma, started up a sting in Duzmut's eyes. At which, she footed it out of the grotto.

She knew what to do.

Back at the main hall, she saw fear had its claws in most of those inside. They shrank from the noise of vultures on the roof and crawled under holy furniture. Rooves, walls: like she might have told them, once you hide in them you can't come out again. That's why townspeople lack confidence.

Duzmut threw instructions. "Qip, I need camel's piss. Pails of camel's piss. You know where to stick your elbow in a camel bladder? Yoshet, can you venture outside with me? There's a type of

47

onion called corpse's tears—strong enough to make a corpse cry—that's rarely far from rhubarb. I need a sack of them."

The three vultures had gouged a hole and were obviously set on getting in. They didn't let themselves be distracted by Duzmut and Yoshet slipping out the gate.

Where Duzmut pulled onions, a fourth vulture found them. This one walked on human legs—on a man chopped at the waist. Perhaps waist-down was too much human, for the amalgam didn't want to fly. It ran at Yoshet with its bird legs and feet stuck out like arms with grapples. Yoshet howled in its face and danced insanely rearwards of his sword, which did deter the bird until Duzmut came at it from the side and heaved a soft blow on feathers. The feathers' undercoat of down, inches thick, sank strokes the way felt armour did. Yoshet crouched and went after its outsized dangly tackle between the legs. Its bottom half of human, they smelt from up this close, gave off the fetor of a two-day corpse and bulged with gas. Stomach hollow, Duzmut saw Yoshet miss his swing—maybe he underestimated his sensory disgust. The bird caught him up in its feet-arms.

Duzmut leapt onto its back. When a tree has the only greenery in sight a goat can jump up to a puzzlingly high branch, and so she did. She sawed her sword at its scraggy camel-neck. Like a goat she balanced through its lunges and the gusts from its enormous flapping wings. She slid her legs apart to sit astride its neck and slit its gizzard.

Yoshet had punctures in his boiled leather vest. But his greatcoat, felted yak hair waterproofed with sheep grease, was ready to withstand worse, he claimed. It didn't have to on the rest of their excursion, Yoshet with the sack of onions, Duzmut with her sword out.

The onions, chopped in quarters, immediately wept a pungent juice. Tossed into the camel's piss, the pails bubbled up and hissed. Duzmut said, "Follow me and do as I do."

Duzmut, Qip, and Yoshet, toddling with two pails each, went at something of a run up the path. Inside the grotto, Duzmut splashed her potion, still hissing, onto the frescoed walls. Right away, paint blistered and came off in flakes. Qip threw her pails over paintwork farther in. Yoshet suffered a moment's consternation—this was sacred art—before he did his part in the defacement.

"Now lay low," Angaj-Duzmut told her friends, and they dropped to the ground.

The spirits of the tortured—captured in these images like flies stuck in a web, like birds limed on a twig—struggled loose. The hell scenes that affixed them fell to crumbs. Above Duzmut where she lay, they batted from wall to wall—she felt the rush—in a fraught murmur of confusion. That wail had cut off. Mad spirits might tear her friends to pieces or touch their minds and send them mad likewise. Duzmut kept her eyes on the cave floor. As a pressure of the air, an oppression of her soul she felt their presence, and thus she felt them leave. They whooshed through the cracks to the daylight.

The three friends walked back down the path. No vultures on the roof. In the sky, a flock of them, high up and flying east.

Nothing hindered their exit from the abandoned temple. They were haggard, but they were whole, and had tucked the fly whisk and the bell in their baggage just in case.

Angaj-Duzmut turned to look at the big gilt inscription over the gate. "What does it say?"

The trader read to her. "Temple of Punitive Compassion."

"Is that a temple name?" Lhazo wrinkled his nose. "More suits an arch of triumph."

Arches of triumph were found around the state's frontiers or once-frontiers. Every major road led you through them. Erected in conquest days or after 'bandit cleansings', which meant any put-down of revolt. Lhazo was right, that was the style of their dedicatory inscriptions: Arch of Savages Who Have Learned Docility, Arch of the King's Love Upon Misguided Rebels.

An irritating rain continued on the otherwise quiet hillside.

At the end of the job, the group enjoyed a feast laid on by Qip's four wives. The wives drove four tent-carts, where Qip lived when not on hire. The carts had traversed vast spaces, and each wife had an adventurous tale about how she yoked her fortunes to the convoy.

Afterwards Angaj-Duzmut took her wages back into the bandits' Commonwealth. She had earned more cash than she had ever owned in total and didn't even know where to stash it. Probably she'd buy a horse, but for now went on her legs as she was used to. In concession to the weight of brass she did purchase a donkey and loaded him with a luxury of waterskins as well. Tame donkeys had nothing of their wild cousin's relish but were a kind of fusion of boiled boot and wet felt. He was safe.

The Utszu of the Scarlet Jackets met her with a comrade's hug, and at night a kiss.

Nobody went by their names here. Gangs took waterbird aliases in the marshes, so the Scarlet Jackets were the Wild Geese Gang and their king the Goose Utszu. Angaj-Duzmut couldn't object when she lost her two-parts Black Tents name and became Goatskin Duzmut, or often only Goatskin.

Goatskin told the Goose Utszu her tale of the temple in the rhubarb hills nearby. When she reached her desecration of the grotto with camel's piss and corpse's-tears onion juice, the Goose king laughed.

Her laughter, as Goatskin Duzmut had early on observed, was off-putting to her own, much as her gang admired her. From earthly throat, Duzmut had never heard a laugh that so spilt like chaos through the cracks of the self-evident, self-satisfied—of the settled. It was a spirit's gift, that laughter.

When she finished, she asked Goatskin Duzmut, "Did you know the artist of those frescoes is revered, two hundred years on, considered the finest religious artist in the history of the Great State White and High?"

"If this is true," asked Goatskin Duzmut in return, "why paint between the salt marshes and the steppe, in a place that must always have been desolate—by the standards of the state?"

"Because those slopes saw the last resistance to the state two hundred years ago. My marshes were a shelter before the Commonwealth existed. Fighters against the conquest gathered here. And when they lost their last battle, executions were held as a great public spectacle. The temple commemorates those."

"As scenes of hell?"

"Where else is punishment righteous but in hell and at the hands of the public executioner? My gang," the Utszu went on, "has fifteen and upwards members with those telltale injuries, stigmata inflicted by the magistrates. Mine, too, listened to atrocity legitimated, as in the temples you can hear that a cosmos needs its dungeons."

The Utszu got it. Bandits were village folk for the most part—not tribals, not Qiang, the grab-name for local peoples westwards of Fattimbet, most nomad.

But Goatskin Duzmut hadn't known the history of these marshes as a refuge for Qiang like herself in resistance to the conquest state two hundred years ago. The Utszu and she had this ground in common.

"What about the vultures? Were they the eaters of the dead from that last battle?"

"From the executions," answered the Utszu. "For the tale goes, the corpses were laid out for the birds of the air to do them the holy last rites. But after the vultures had eaten, they were slaughtered. Soldiers went in and the glutted birds, too fat to fly, were massacred themselves. They had been polluted with traitors to the state." She wondered for a moment, her dark gaze on Angaj-Duzmut. "You have let a flock loose. A flock of..."

The Utszu didn't know. At least she didn't, by default, call them demons. "Unhappy spirits." Angaj-Duzmut gave her understanding. "Haunt-spirits. I let them loose, but I cannot set them free. Only a great shaman can console and cure an unhappy spirit of its hurt. Until then, they are wildly dangerous. They can cause plagues or slay as wantonly as any army."

"If that is true"—the Utszu stretched her arms, strong fingers in the inch of black hair on her head—"and they flew east, I hope they fly a thousand miles to Irighaya, and make a visit to the king."

The Utszu and Goatskin Duzmut sat together by a lake in the blaze of a low sun. As they watched, wild geese rose off the water with loud celebratory flapping, to wheel and whirl for the sheer excitement of the thing.

ABOUT THE AUTHOR

Bryn Hammond (she/her) writes the *Amgalant* series, historical fiction on the life of Chinggis Khan. *Voices from the Twelfth-Century Steppe* discusses her creative engagement with her primary source, the *Secret History of the Mongols*. Work in *The Knot Wound Round Your Finger* from Bell Press, *Lothlorien Poetry Journal*, *Ergot.*, *Queer Weird West Tales* ed. Julie Bozza. Bryn is queer (lesbian, ex-bisexual, slides more towards trans than cis – it's complicated). She lives in a coastal town in Australia, where she likes to write while walking in the sea.

www.amgalant.com
@Jakujin

The Origin of the New Edge

Howard Andrew Jones

Around the turn of the millennium Daniel Blackston asked me if I wanted to run a Sword & Sorcery e-zine sponsored by Pitch-Black Books, a creation of Blackston and Dave Pitchford. At the time, Sword & Sorcery was even harder to get into print than it is today. A lot of magazines, both real world and online, claimed to accept it, but only *Black Gate* really did with any regularity, and, unfortunately, *Black Gate*'s publication schedule was glacial.

So, when it was announced that our little *Flashing Swords* e-zine was going to be devoted to Sword & Sorcery, it's no wonder our one-cent-a-word publication ended up with a selection of exceptional Sword & Sorcery stories. Some of the first stories I pulled out of the submission pile were from Warhammer writers William King and Clint Werner. Correspondences developed quickly between John C. Hocking and us, and we got to brainstorming about what we wanted to see in a world we hoped would one day be more interested in publishing Sword & Sorcery.

Naturally, we craved more markets so we could read more new stories and have places to publish what we were creating. We were all disappointed that high fantasy and urban fantasy and gaming fiction fantasy (and cat fantasy, etc.) were everywhere but that so few places wanted to give what we loved any room. In those days, the term Sword & Sorcery hadn't yet gotten as confused as it has today (almost to the point of irrelevance, I'm afraid, but that's a topic for a whole different essay). Instead, owing to a glut of cheesy Sword & Sorcery movies and C-grade Clonans, popular conception had

it that all Sword & Sorcery, even those tales by Robert E. Howard himself, was nothing but stories about grunting, fur-diaper-wearing barbarians. It was easier to find comic send-ups of Sword & Sorcery than it was the real thing.

The four of us tossed around some ideas to describe things we were already trying to do in our fiction, and that we saw other people doing in theirs, and decided that The New Edge was a decent name for it. My thinking was if there could be a New Weird and a New Wave, why not a New Edge?

In a series of essays inside the e-zine, I wrote about four major points.

1. We can find inspiration from the old tales without pastiching them. Specifically, setting aside the sexism and racism and the suspect politics but embracing the virtues of great pulp storytelling. The color. The pace. The headlong thrill and sense of wonder. The celebration not of the everyday and the petty but of those who dare to fight on when the odds are against them.

2. We can create new characters, not homages or ironic sendups.

3. We can craft fascinating, living settings as in not faux REH or generic game fiction backdrop number nine. We need to make our own worlds and look past the seemingly unbreakable molds set in place by the big names and the gaming manuals.

4. We must restore the sense of the fantastic. Once magic is banal or easy, once magic rings can be found at the corner market and wizards are everywhere, sense of wonder goes straight out the window.

With the editorials came some spirited discussion about the New Edge at the wonderful Pitch-Black forum, and then, well, then it suddenly was all over. My involvement with the e-zine concluded after the first six issues. I ended up working for *Black Gate* for many years before joining forces with *Tales from the Magician's Skull* and, at some point in there, launching a novel career.

I'm still on board with most of the essay, but I see now that we weren't really starting a movement so much as labeling something that was already under development. I was younger and angrier and a little too focused on some of my points and oblivious to some additional good ones that could have been made. I most regret sounding completely down on homage or pastiche, the best examples of which can be a blast, and I've since read some pretty great game fiction. But in my defense, at that time, a lot of bad homage and pastiche was dragging the genre down, and standard gaming fiction could be found everywhere while what we loved was absent.

These days a lot of the obstacles seem to be dropping by the wayside. We're living in an exciting age for Sword & Sorcery. More and more online and physical venues are welcoming to our long-neglected subgenre, and great small press firms are giving voice to new writers and reprinting lost classics. A major publisher has just made a serious commitment to publishing a whole new set of Sword & Sorcery writers, and I'm delighted to be one of them. If I'd been told twenty years ago that I'd be editing a Sword & Sorcery magazine and signing a five-book hardback deal of interconnected Sword & Sorcery titles, my jaw would have dropped open in wonder.

I still love the concept of shaking the rust off an old blade and putting a new edge to it. The idea seems to resonate with a lot of people, some of whom will take it to mean more, or less, or even slightly different things than I do. So be it. I think that means the movement is real and growing. My sincerest hope is that it will never become one of the dividing lines we keep tripping over and that the New Edge instead remains a campfire around which we can gather and share the kind of fiction we love.

Howard Andrew Jones' Ring-Sworn trilogy and his two historical Arabian fantasy novels from St. Martin's were critically acclaimed by *Publishers Weekly* and other review outlets. He was the driving force behind the rebirth of interest in Harold Lamb's historical fiction, and assembled and edited eight collections of Lamb's work for the University of Nebraska Press. He is the editor for the Sword & Sorcery magazine *Tales from the Magician's Skull* and served as Managing Editor of *Black Gate* magazine. He lurks at www.howard andrewjones.com, where he blogs about writing craft, gaming, fantasy and adventure fiction, and assorted nerdery.

C.L. Moore and Jirel of Joiry:
The First Lady of Sword & Sorcery
Cora Buhlert

The claim that Sword & Sorcery is an inherently masculine genre that women neither read nor write rears its ugly head with depressing regularity. This claim could not be more wrong, because many women have contributed to Sword & Sorcery as writers, editors, and artists since the genre was born in the pages of *Weird Tales* more than ninety years ago. Indeed, women have been a part of Sword & Sorcery since the very beginning.

Hereby, two women whose works appeared in the pages of *Weird Tales* in the 1930s stand out: cover artist Margaret Brundage, who illustrated many a Conan story and was one of the first artists to depict the Cimmerian barbarian, and C. L. Moore, the first woman to write Sword & Sorcery and creator of the first female Sword & Sorcery heroine Jirel of Joiry.

Catherine Lucille Moore was born in 1911 in Indianapolis. A lifelong reader of science fiction and fantasy, she published a few stories in *The Vagabond*, the student magazine of the University of Indiana. During the Great Depression, Moore had to leave college and started working as a secretary at the bank *Fletcher Trust Company* in Indianapolis to support her family. While practicing typing after hours at

the bank, she wrote what would become her first professionally published story and submitted it to *Weird Tales* under her initials C. L. Moore, because she feared she would lose her job at the bank, should her extracurricular writing activities become known. Moore's story impressed editor Farnsworth Wright so much that he bought it on the spot for the then princely sum of one hundred dollars.

The story in question, "Shambleau" introduced the interplanetary outlaw Northwest Smith to the world. A prototype for space rogues such as Han Solo of *Star Wars* fame or Malcolm Reynolds from *Firefly*, Northwest Smith was named after a customer at the *Fletcher Trust Company*, one N. W. Smith, while the name of his Venusian friend Yarol is an anagram of the *Royal* typewriter Moore used at the bank.

"Shambleau" opens in a frontier town on Mars, where Northwest Smith rescues a young woman from a mob intent on killing her and takes her back to his apartment. However, the woman turns out to be a Shambleau, a member of a medusa-like alien species. Smith only narrowly escapes her addictive tentacled embrace.

"Shambleau" was an instant sensation when it appeared in the November 1933 issue of *Weird Tales*. It was one of the most popular stories published in *Weird Tales* during the tenure of Farnsworth Wright, second only to "The Three Marked Pennies" by Mary Elizabeth Counselman, and remains one of Moore's best-known stories, reprinted more than thirty times in the past ninety years. Three further

Northwest Smith stories followed in rapid succession in 1934.

Though set on Mars and Venus, the Northwest Smith tales could not be more different from the gadget-focussed science fiction found in magazines like *Amazing Stories, Astounding Stories,* or *Wonder Stories.* Northwest Smith is no heroic inventor or interplanetary patrolman who tackles scientific mysteries. Instead, he is an outlaw and a wanderer, closer to Conan than to Richard Seaton from the *Skylark* novels by E. E. Smith. Nor does Northwest Smith heroically rescue nubile maidens from the slimy embrace of bug-eyed monsters. Instead, the beautiful women Smith meets are either doomed or they are monsters themselves. Smith usually barely escapes with his life.

The Northwest Smith stories are also as sexually charged as the strict standards of the pulp era permitted. "Shambleau" culminates in two and a half pages of what is essentially a drug trip-cum-sex scene with a tentacled alien woman. The 1935 story "Julhi" opens with a lovingly detailed description of every single scar on Northwest Smith's body, and he has a lot of them. Coincidentally, Smith is described as brown-skinned in this and other stories, i.e., he is one of the comparatively few characters of colour to be found in speculative fiction in the 1930s and 1940s.

One last thing that sets Moore's work apart from other science fiction writers of the period is the dreamlike atmosphere. Northwest Smith tends to stumble into fantastic and nigh hallucinogenic realms straight out of a Clark Ashton Smith story and faces horrors that would not be out of place in any H. P. Lovecraft tale.

After a string of Northwest Smith stories, C. L. Moore turned her talent to Sword & Sorcery and created the budding genre's first female protagonist with the French medieval swordswoman Jirel of Joiry.

Jirel burst onto the scene in the October 1934 issue of *Weird Tales* in the story "Black God's Kiss." In the much-imitated opening scene, Jirel is brought in full armour before Guillaume, the enemy knight who has conquered her castle. Her helmet is pulled off and her gender revealed, a revelation that would have had even more impact if cover artist Margaret Brundage and interior artist Hugh Rankin had not spoiled it.

Jirel's introduction is not the first time a supposedly male knight is revealed to be a woman underneath the armour. A similar revelation occurs in Robert E. Howard's historical adventure story "The Sowers of the Thunder", published in the winter 1932 issue of *Weird Tales'* sister magazine *Oriental Stories,* where a crusader known only as the Masked Knight is revealed to be a woman shortly before dying in her former lover's arms. But while the revelation of the true identity of the Masked Knight in "The Sowers of the Thunder" is a throwaway scene, Moore puts the revelation of Jirel's gender front and centre. Every scene in popular culture, where the mask, hood, or helmet of a seemingly male or genderless figure is removed to reveal an attractive woman, can be traced back to Jirel of Joiry.

The Jirel of Joiry stories are as sexually charged as the Northwest Smith stories. Jirel is no wilting virgin, but a sexually experienced woman, something that would have been shocking even decades later. However, the Jirel stories also deal with the darker side of sexuality in the form of sexual assault, a subject that occasionally appears in Sword & Sorcery. For example, some of the Conan stories touch on sexual violence, though contrary to popular belief, Conan himself does not commit sexual assault. "Black God's Kiss," however, centres the subject of sexual assault—represented here by Guillaume forcing a kiss on Jirel, since the censorship standards of the time would not allow for anything more explicit—and the resulting trauma in a way no other Sword & Sorcery story has done before and few since.

The bulk of "Black God's Kiss" follows Jirel as she passes through a portal deep underneath Castle Joiry into a hellish realm that is highly reminiscent of Lovecraft's Dreamlands. Here, Jirel seeks a weapon to avenge herself on Guillaume, while keeping her soul and sanity intact. Jirel succeeds, too, and destroys Guillaume with a deadly kiss. However, there is a cost, for Jirel's feelings for Guillaume are more complicated than she dares to admit. And so, in the sequel "Black God's Shadow," published in the December 1934 issue of *Weird Tales,* Jirel returns to the nightmarish realm underneath Castle Joiry, this time to free Guillaume's soul from the curse she placed upon him.

Many readers tend to approach the Jirel of Joiry stories expecting a sword-swinging female Conan, but that is not who Jirel is. Instead, the Jirel stories focus on journeys through nightmarish lands, which serve as a metaphor for Jirel's psychological journey as a survivor of sexual assault. It is certainly no accident that of the six stories about Jirel that appeared in *Weird Tales,* four feature Jirel facing off against overbearing men and braving nightmarish horrors in order to free herself from their influence.

"Black God's Kiss" was voted the most popular story in the October 1934 issue of *Weird Tales,* beating even "People of the Black Circle," one of Robert E. Howard's best Conan stories. Indeed, the Jirel of Joiry stories

were popular with the readers of *Weird Tales*, as letters to "The Eyrie" prove, belying the claim that Sword & Sorcery fans did not want to read stories about female protagonists. Even the much-quoted letter to "The Eyrie" by one Bert Felsburg from Frackville, Pennsylvania, who complained about the lack of action in "Black God's Kiss," while professing his love for Conan and Northwest Smith, is put into perspective, once you realise that Bert Felsburg was only fourteen years old when he wrote that letter.

But it wasn't just regular readers who enjoyed C. L. Moore's stories. Fans of her work included such *Weird Tales* stalwarts as H. P. Lovecraft, Robert E. Howard, and Robert Bloch. Lovecraft called Moore "one of the greatest talents in *Weird Tales*" and kept up a lively correspondence with her from 1935 to his death in 1937. Robert Bloch, who famously disliked Conan, very much enjoyed the Jirel stories, as he wrote in a letter to "The Eyrie." Robert E. Howard also struck up a correspondence with C. L. Moore and sent her the

manuscript of "Sword Woman," a story about Dark Agnes de Chastillon, Howard's own warrior heroine, which never saw publication during his lifetime.

Another fan of C. L. Moore was Henry Kuttner, a young *Weird Tales* reader and aspiring writer. Kuttner was another correspondent of H.P. Lovecraft's, and his first few stories were strongly inspired by Lovecraft's work. Lovecraft encouraged Kuttner to write to C. L. Moore, which Kuttner promptly did in February 1936, addressing his letter to "Dear Mr. Moore," since

53

Moore's gender, though revealed in the fanzine *The Fantasy Fan* in 1934, was not yet widely known at the time. Moore cleared up the error and the two began corresponding and collaborating on "Quest of the Starstone," the 1937 story which brought together Jirel of Joiry and Northwest Smith. It would be the first of many collaborations.

In 1940, Kuttner and Moore married. Most of their stories written after this point were collaborations. According to L. Sprague De Camp, when one of them would get up from the typewriter to get a cup of coffee, go grocery shopping and make dinner, the other would sit down and continue writing where the first left off, often mid-paragraph or even mid-sentence.

Around the time they got married, Kuttner and Moore also both abandoned *Weird Tales*, the magazine that had given them their start, for higher paying markets. Moore's last story for *Weird Tales* was "Hellsgarde," published in the April 1939 issue of *Weird Tales*, which sends Jirel of Joiry into a haunted castle on a quest to free her captured men from a villainous warlord. The last story by Kuttner to appear in *Weird Tales* was "Dragon Moon," an adventure of Kuttner's Sword & Sorcery hero Elak of Atlantis, which appeared in the January 1941 issue.

Along with *Weird Tales*, Kuttner and Moore also left the fading Sword & Sorcery genre behind and turned their attention to science fiction, which was more popular and paid better. From the early 1940s on, Kuttner and Moore appeared regularly in John W. Campbell's sister magazines *Astounding Science Fiction* and *Unknown*, at the time the highest paying markets for speculative fiction, often under joint pen names such as Lewis Padgett, C. H. Liddell or Lawrence O'Donnell. In 1943, Kuttner and Moore

even managed to break into *Argosy*, at the time one of the highest paying and most prestigious pulp magazines.

Throughout the 1940s and 1950s, C. L. Moore continued to write outstanding fiction, both together with Kuttner and on her own, such as "The Twonky," "Mimsy Were the Borogroves," "The Children's Hour," "Vintage Season," "Judgment Night," or "No Woman Born," though those stories tend to lack the raw power of the Northwest Smith and Jirel of Joiry stories.

C. L. Moore was one of the best writers of the so-called golden age of science fiction, yet she is rarely mentioned in the same breath as Isaac Asimov, Robert A. Heinlein or A. E. Van Vogt, whose work appeared alongside hers in the pages of *Astounding*. The fact that later reprints often attributed collaborative stories solely to Henry Kuttner did not help either.

In 1956, C.L. Moore became one of the first two women (the other was Leigh Brackett, nominated in the same year for the novel The Long Tomorrow) to be nominated for the Hugo Award together with Henry Kuttner for the novelette "Home There's No Returning". Though Hugo glory would elude Kuttner and Moore until 2018 and 2019, when "The Twonky" and "Mimsy Were the Borogroves" won the 1943 and 1944 Retro Hugo respectively.

Moore's personal life was not without tragedy. In 1936, her fiancé, a fellow employee at the *Fletcher Trust Company*, died of a self-inflicted gunshot wound. Her marriage to Henry Kuttner, while happy, remained childless since Moore suffered several miscarriages. In 1958, finally, tragedy struck again, when Henry Kuttner died of a heart attack, aged only 42.

By this time, both Moore and Kuttner were already moving away from writing and had gone

back to university to get their degrees. After Kuttner's death, Moore taught creative writing at the University of Southern California and worked for a few years as a television screenwriter under her married name Catherine Kuttner. She remarried in 1963 and stopped writing fiction altogether.

However, Moore continued to attend conventions and late in life, she gained the recognition that had eluded her during her active period. In 1980, she received the World Fantasy Convention Lifetime Achievement Award and the following year the Gandalf Grand Master Award. C. L. Moore was also named Science Fiction and Fantasy Writers of America Grand Master, the first woman writer to be so honoured, but because she had developed Alzheimer's disease by this point, her second husband declined the honour on her behalf. Moore died in 1987, aged 76.

In the mid 1960s, the *Lancer Conan* reprints and the first paperback publication of *The Lord of the Rings* kicked the budding Sword & Sorcery revival into overdrive and brought many long forgotten tales of the first Sword & Sorcery boom back into print. And so, the *Jirel of Joiry* stories were collected and reprinted in 1969 and have remained in print almost continuously since then. But while C. L. Moore was one of the few writers of the original Sword & Sorcery boom of the 1930s who was still alive—the only other survivor of that era was Fritz Leiber—she never revisited Jirel.

As a result, those six stories from the 1930s are all we have of Jirel of Joiry. And while the adventures of Conan or Fafhrd and Gray Mouser span roughly thirty years of their lives, Jirel's adventures take place over a fairly short period of time. This does not mean that Jirel does not change or develop over the course of her adventures, but her journey is psychological and focusses on Jirel coming to terms with the sexual assault she experienced and her complicated feelings for Guillaume. All this contributes to the fact that the Jirel of Joiry stories do not get nearly as much attention as they deserve.

But even though there only are a handful of Jirel of Joiry stories, C. L. Moore and the medieval swordswoman she created left a lasting impact on the Sword & Sorcery genre and popular culture in general.

C. L. Moore's work directly influenced her contemporaries. Leigh Brackett was not only a personal friend of Moore's, but her 1951 sword and planet adventure "Black Amazon of Mars" can be viewed as an attempt to rewrite "Black God's Kiss" with a happier ending. And while Robert E. Howard had already been experimenting with writing about woman warriors—*Bêlit* from "Queen of the Black Coast," the Masked Knight from "The Sowers of the Thunder" and the original Red Sonya of Rogatino from "The Shadow of the Vulture" all predate Jirel—the Jirel of Joiry stories proved that there was a market for stories about warrior woman. Would we have Valeria of the Red Brotherhood from "Red Nails" if not for Jirel?

C. L. Moore also influenced future generations of writers. She blazed the trail for women writers of Sword & Sorcery who came along during the second Sword & Sorcery boom in the 1960s and 1970s such as Tanith Lee, Jessica Amanda Salmonson, Joanna Russ, Janet Morris, Sharon Green, Pat Macintosh, or Jennifer Roberson.

Meanwhile, Jirel herself was the prototype for many a warrior heroine. Charles R. Saunders's Dossouye is his answer to Jirel just as Imaro was Saunders's answer to Conan. The Marvel Comics version of Red Sonja may be nominally based on a Robert E. Howard character, but owes as much to Jirel of Joiry, including a backstory of sexual assault, as to Howard's Red Sonya of Rogatino. And pop culture heroines like *Xena: Warrior Princess*, Teela from *He-Man and the Masters of the Universe* or *She-Ra: Princess of Power* are all spiritual granddaughters of Jirel of Joiry.

Even though the Jirel of Joiry stories are almost ninety years old by now, they still hold up and are well worth reading for every Sword & Sorcery fan and for everybody interested in the history of women in science fiction and fantasy.

Cora Buhlert was born and bred in Bremen, North Germany, where she still lives today – after time spent in London, Singapore, Rotterdam and Mississippi. Cora holds an MA degree in English from the University of Bremen.

Cora has been writing since she was a teenager, and has published stories, articles and poetry in various international magazines. She is the author of the Silencer series of pulp style thrillers, the Shattered Empire space opera series, the In Love and War science fiction romance series, the Thurvok and Kurval sword and sorcery series, the Helen Shepherd Mysteries and plenty of standalone stories in multiple genres. Cora is the winner of the 2022 Hugo Award for Best Fan Writer and the 2021 Space Cowboy Award. When Cora is not writing, she works as a translator and teacher.

www.corabuhlert.com
@CoraBuhlert

Sword & Soul: An Interview with Milton Davis

NOTE: This interview originally aired on October 25, 2021 as episode twenty of the podcast *So I'm Writing a Novel...* hosted by Oliver Brackenbury. This transcript has been edited for length.

INTRO: As part of my research in trying to become more familiar with the Sword & Sorcery genre, I discovered what is referred to as 'Sword & Soul.' Sword & Soul means Sword & Sorcery stories focusing on tales of people of colour with semi-historical or full-on fictional settings rooted in African History, cultures, and myths. I think it's fair to say it was born out of the work 'Imaro' by Charles Saunders and, in studying Saunders and learning about him, my attention was drawn to a contemporary writer named Milton J. Davis, with whom I will be speaking today.

Milton is a Speculative Fiction writer but also a publisher, as owner of MVmedia, a small publishing company specialising in Science Fiction, Fantasy, and Sword & Soul. Their mission is to provide Speculative Fiction books that represent people of colour in a positive manner.

As an author, he has written 21 novels and short story collections, his most recent being a Sword & Soul adventure called *Eda Blessed II*. He is also a contributing author to *Black Panther: Tales of Wakanda*, published by Marvel and TIME Books, and co-author of *Hadithi & the State of Black Speculative Fiction* with Eugene Bacon.

There is a great deal more he has done as Editor as well, but I think the best thing to do is to get into it and let Milton tell you about himself.

OLIVER: And here we are with Milton Davis. Hi, Milton.

MILTON: Hey, how you doin', man?

O: Pretty good. All right. Especially now that I got rid of the cat that just made that noise. But anyway. (*laughing*) It's pretty professional over here.

Let's get into it. Okay, so, going as far back as you can remember, what is your, sort of, the earliest reading experience you had that led to your lifetime love of Fantasy fiction.

M: Well, it's interesting because, initially, I did not read a lot of Fantasy in fiction. I used to be a big History reader. Any experience I had with Fantasy came through what my cousin - my cousin was a big comic book reader - and I guess my first introduction to Fantasy was the Conan series that Marvel did.

But it wasn't until I was in college that I actually started reading Science Fiction and Fantasy. And that was because I had a college instructor – I was a Chemistry major – and I had an English class and I did my first essay and my instructor, Anna Holloway, who's a friend of mine now, called me to her office and said, 'Well, why are you majoring in Chemistry? You're a good writer.' And I said 'Well, writers don't make any money.' And I've proven that over the years. (*laughing*)

But anyway, she was the person who actually introduced me to Science Fiction and Fantasy. I think it was, since I was a Science major, I think that was her way to get me interested in writing by introducing me to something that she felt was connected to what I was majoring in. And so, it was initially people like Asimov and Arthur C. Clark and Heinlein and Samuel Delany But eventually started going into, you know, some of the Fantasy authors like, Robert E. Howard, Michael Moorecock, you know, different things like that. That's what really kinda got me into it.

O: Cool. Now I'm going to be that guy. I'm curious, do you remember what the Marvel Conans - was that the sort of mainstream Marvel line? Or was it the *Savage Sword of Conan* magazine size guys that were always in black & white?

M: It was those *Savage Sword of Conans* – those and the comic book, as well. I read both of them. You know, of course there was movies. I grew up in the 60s, so I'm watching, you know, everything like that to me was mainly visual. I was really into, like, Jason and the Argonauts and stuff like that, so I guess I would consider that my introduction to Fantasy as well but it was mostly visual. It wasn't the written word.

O: I would love to hear your definition of Sword & Soul. How would you define that?

M: Well, to me, Sword & Soul is basically a fantasy, epic fantasy, Sword & Sorcery that's based on pre-colonial African culture and tradition and history. That's basically what it is, in a nutshell.

O: You've published other things, but I feel like that's your 'flagship' genre within MVmedia. What's it like being both a writer and a publisher? Like, when you submit your stories to people, does your publishing side make you want to dispute any rejections you get a little more, like, being both the referee and the player? (*laughing*) How does that go?

M: I think it makes me more sympathetic to people who submit stuff to me because, as a writer as well, I always understand what they're going through and I think it makes me kind of a 'softie' because I've been on the other end of it.

But, once I started self-publishing, once I started indie publishing, I really don't submit - very rarely do I submit something to magazines or other publications. It's usually by request. Someone will get into contact with me and say, 'Hey, Milton, I've got this anthology coming up and I wanted to know' – it'd be either, 'Can you write a story for it?' Or, 'I read this story that you wrote and I want to know if I can use this in that anthology.' And, I guess, for me the pressure isn't there as far as submitting because I am an indie publisher – I know my stuff is going to get published one way or another. (*laughing*)

O: My apologies – of course there are people approaching you. You don't have to audition anymore! (*laughing*) We're at that level of the career. My apologies. Speaking of publishing, I mean, you've been doing it for a while, right? Like, sixteen years, if I'm correct?

M: Well, actually thirteen years. I started writing in 2005. Then I decided I was going do this thing and I was going to do it indie and it took me about three years to write enough, to have enough content, to where I started publishing. I wanted to let out at least one book every year. So, I wanted to build enough backlog to where I wouldn't be writing on the next book for that next year, I always had to be two or three books ahead. So when that year came 'round, I could just say 'Okay, we'll roll this book out.' I'm working on Book Four while Book One is being released, that kind of thing. So, that was my plan going into it.

O: All right. That's work ethic, man. I'd love to get out one book a year, geeze.

I'm wondering, if you could travel back in time and talk to your 2008 self, what would you tell them that you've learned in publishing? You know, to save them some grief. What lessons would you pass back to yourself?

M: I would tell them that 'your business projections are wrong.' (*laughing*) That's what I would tell them. But, you know, there's really not much I would change. I was very fortunate that, when I got into it, I decided to do indie publishing after studying the market. And I really had a feeling that what I was trying to write was not going to be very acceptable to publishing the way it was at the time. And that's one of the reasons I decided to go independent. I also wanted the freedom to write stories the way I wanted to write them. Without any kind of input. And all that just came down to being an indie publisher. I was fortunate, when I decided to do it, that I ran into people who were experienced at doing that and they gave me very good advice on how to get started. It helped me avoid some of the pitfalls that people run into when they're doing indie publishing - like, bad editors and, you know, people that tell you they're doing to 'do this' and never do it. That kind of thing. And they gave me context that helped me get into the whole process very easily. So, I don't have too many regrets about it. I think, based on what I was available to do at the time, I just started where I could and just worked my way to this point.

O: Is there any one piece of advice or lesson you'd want to pay forward to anybody who's looking to start up their own company now?

M: I would just say, do the re-

search. And understand that, when you become a self-publisher, indie publisher, you are basically going into business. Because, you have to do everything yourself and you're responsible for everything. And you have to go at it with that kind of a work ethic. Nobody is really going to do anything for you. You have to be able to do your marketing, your cover design, your editing, you have to pay editors, all that stuff you have to do yourself. I do a class once a year – well, I was doing it once a year until recently – where I would talk to people about self-publishing. And the first question I would ask them was: What do you want to get out of writing? And that will determine whether self-publishing is for you or if you should take another path. Because some people, they just want to write. They don't want to be bothered with all the other stuff. And if that's what you want to do, then, I would tell them, you really need to reconsider becoming an indie publisher. Cause you have to set aside time to do all that other stuff.

O: Yeah. I was just saying in my last interview, to author Jess Frey, we were talking about self-publishing and how you need to be prepared, in the sense that, 'you can do everything, you have total creative control', but you just want to change that tone of voice slightly and be like 'you can do everything! *You do everything.*' (*laughing*)

M: Exactly. Exactly.

O: It's a good thing to keep in mind.

M: Yeah, it is.

O: Okay, so if I understand correctly, part of your literary origin story was meeting and then going on to have had a working relationship with the father of Sword

& Soul, Charles Saunders – author of the magnificent Imaro series, and more. I imagine you would agree with me, that Saunders isn't just noteworthy – he is noteworthy but he is not just noteworthy for being a black, Sword & Sorcery author, writing stories grounded in African culture. He's noteworthy because he was a good writer that brought new depth to his beloved genre. What is something you admire about his writing? About his craft?

M: You said it exactly. The first story I read by him was a story called 'Gimli's Song,' which is in the *Dark Matter Anthology*, which was the first anthology that was created with focusing on Black Speculative Fiction. It was a story about one of his other characters that people don't really know a lot about - her name was Dossouye - and I read the story and I was like 'Man, this is a good story. This guy Charles is pretty good.' But I wasn't really into Fantasy and Science Fiction at the time when I read it. But then, as I was working on my own projects, I was like, somebody has had to do this before because there's just too much stuff out there. And right before I released - I was working on *Mji* - Night Shade re-released their Imaro Series and I was like, okay, yeah, I knew there was somebody else out there and that's when I started reading the stuff. And when I started reading this book - it's just, his story telling ability - and for me, particularly as a writer, his vocabulary, was just blowing me away. And I'm like, this guy must have his own little thesaurus somewhere *(laughing)* that is just for him and he has all these words. And I was just reading his stuff and the depth of his story was a lot different than what I was used to when I read your typical Sword & Sorcery -type books. As I read further on, after we met, and I

started reading more and more of his series, started to go into other books, you could start to see, even from the point that I read it earlier, you could see his craft even getting better and growing to the point by the time you get to Imaro Four – after I read Imaro Four, I told people, I said 'Look, you need to stop comparing Charles Saunders to Robert E. Howard.' Because, in my opinion, he's way beyond that. He's at this point, he's at this style where he's basically, kind of, gotten away from reflecting that traditional Sword & Sorcery where he's really into his own at this point. And most people that I've met in Sword & Sorcery, they have a lot of respect for Charles. One of the reasons that I had an easier intro into the genre, was because of people who were aware of him and what he had done. The fact that he was saying, 'Hey, check this young brother out,' it was like, kind of, giving me some leeway as I got into the genre with my stories.

O: Yeah, and, like, I wish he had had even more recognition. You know? There does seem to be happening with the kind of Sword & Sorcery, dare I tempt fate and say, renaissance we're sort of having? Or, at least there seems to be more air going back in the balloon, you know? You know, the 80s, bad, schlocky movies kind of let it out. He's getting more attention as people are working their way back through the stuff and then finding out. I've just started Imaro 2 and, yeah, I can already tell like, even by the end, near the end of *Imaro*, the first one, you can see, as you say, him evolving to more his own thing. Obviously he's influenced by Howard, that's where he started, but boy does he just take it beyond. And even in the first book, I love how he gives the character Imaro just a lot more depth. You know, Imaro's kind of

constant search for – trying to find a home and acceptance? And how, at least as far as I've read, it never seems to work out. *(laughing)*

M: I mean, I think that's the thing about Imaro that captures you. Because I've read all of the Conan stories and, you know, Conan's more this barbarian that's kinda just going from adventure to adventure basically, I mean, the running theme across most of Conan's stories is Robert E. Howard showing that sometimes the people that you consider 'uncivilized' are more civilized than the people that are looking down upon them and that kind of thing. But with Imaro, it's more of a personal story. And I think that's what gives it it's depth and and it resonates so much with other peoples because you're actually into – with Conan, I was more looking at 'okay, what's this next adventure going to be?,' you know? 'Who is he going to be fighting next?' That kind of stuff. But with Imaro, I was really into him. Not so much the action but, how is this going to change his life? How is this going to get him closer to what he was searching and seeking and stuff, you know? And I think that's what sets it apart from most of the Sword & Sorcery that you read.

O: Absolutely. And I also admire how - again, I've only just started Book 2 but - what I've read so far, it's like, you have people like Fritz Leiber or Moorcock who would stitch together short stories they had written with no intent to create a saga later in their careers. This seams it would kind of show – I mean, great writers, but still – you know, or have people who picked up Howard's work – you know, Carter and De Camp there in the sixties with their controversial answers, collection of Conan, where they wrote their own stuff to fill in the gaps and so on and so forth...

M: Yeah.

O: But then you read Imaro and he's starting out already with a vision in place, it feels, and I feel – I think, from the first book at least, you can pick out many of the stories and enjoy them on their own even though there is continuity but they, of course, reward you reading them in order. So, it just shows this level of skill that - you don't find it too often.

M: That's true. And you see it too in the collection that we have, *Nyumbani Tales*, which is a collection of his short stories that he wrote over the years and got published in different magazines. None of those stories have Imaro as a main character. But they talk about the world in Nyumbani but even the separate of stories that he tells, in those stories you actually see an underlying theme in all those stories, as well. And as I read each story I was like, okay, there's a theme that comes up in most of Charles's stories and once you read enough of his work you start to see it there. And when you get to know him, and I'm fortunate that I did get a chance to get to know him, you kind of – like most writers, you see where that theme came from. A lot of times it's reflections of your own personal life that you do consciously – or unconsciously – when you write your stories.

O: So, Charles's writing needs to be discussed more, I think we'll both agree on that. But you were lucky enough to be friends with the man. I'm curious, is there anything fun you could tell us just about who he was as a guy? Are there any stories to share?

M: Yeah, he was – I think we hit it off. I met him through a friend of mine who had decided to publish Charles's books after Night Shade started to drop the series. Actually, when I read the Night Shade books, I was trying to get in contact with him. Me, in my naïve self, thought I could just get in contact with a publisher and they would give me his information. When my friend announced that he was going to be picking up the book series, I said, 'Hey man, is there some kind of way you can introduce me to Charles? I'd really like to meet him.' And he did, we met through email. Unfortunately, I never got a chance to meet with him face-to-face. I found out that Charles had a lot of relationships like that, where he was communicating with people long-distance and stuff. But, he read my book, he liked it. And so we started talking and, I think part of it had to do with, our journey had a lot in common. We both were inspired by Robert E. Howard's works, we both chose to use pre-colonial Africa as our foundation for our stories, we were both influenced by some of the same regions in Africa, and the same history. Like, his book *Dossouye* was based on the Meno – the people called the Black Amazons – from Dahomey. And I had actually come up with an idea for my book 'Woman of Woods,' which was based on the same region for the same reasons and stuff. Just separately. We were both born – our birthdays were, like, three days apart. You know, eleven years apart but three days apart in July. We were both Pittsburgh Steelers fans. We both went to historically black colleges. So, it was just like, all this stuff was just, you know.

O: It was meant to be.

M: We just kept running into – there were so many things we had in common and I just think that had a lot to do with the fact that we became friends like that. We had a lot of things in common outside of the genre itself. We would talk about football games all the time. He was a big boxing fan. He actually used to write a lot of articles about particular boxing matches and stuff. That's something a lot of people didn't know about him but he was really big into boxing and stuff like that, so. He had a great sense of humour. He had a way of deciding what he would and would not talk about. If I would send him an email about a subject and it was something he really didn't want to discuss, he sent me an email back, he wouldn't even mention it at all. I would say, 'Okay, well Charles didn't really want to talk about this.' But, yeah, it was a great relationship. Again, like I said, the only think I regret is that I never really got a chance to meet him face-to-face. I had planned to travel to Halifax at some point but before I was able to get a chance to do it he passed away. He was an interesting person. He was fun to chat with.

O: Did he ever talk to you about maybe writing some boxing fiction? I have this weird half-memory that -Howard maybe – wrote. 'Cause I know Howard went well out of Sword & Sorcery, as well – he wrote Westerns and everything else. I feel like maybe he did boxing stories. Or did one or two. I feel like there's a connection there somewhere.

M: Well, actually, Charles had a pulp character that he created called *Damballa*. The book was published a few years ago. I can't remember – Ron Fortier's publishing company – Airship 21. And in that story, there's a boxer in there. That's funny because, when Charles first released *Imaro*, they had an issue because the publisher tried to describe them as a 'black Tarzan.' And that had the Edgar R. Burroughs and – I can't remember the name what you would call them today – they rose up... you can't do that. Their estate, they said 'No, we won't let you do that kind of stuff.' So, when he wrote Damballa, he said, 'Well, you know what? I'm actually going to write my version of a black Tarzan.' And that's what Damballa is, really. And, he actually wrote a short Damballa story, then he wrote this novel. And that novel is about, basically, the Germans having this – this is before World War II – having this boxer that they had basically given these celestial abilities to and, in this particular story, Damballa is having to fight this boxer. That's the only fiction story that I know of that he actually incorporated his love of boxing into his fiction.

O: That's so cool, though. And I love how he took, like, the bad marketing he was given and like, 'Alright, I'm going to do something with that.'

M: Yeah, exactly. He said, 'Somebody's claiming that I did it. I'm going to actually do it.'

O: I can respect the hell out of that. I love it.
So, I would say, it's fair to say you have some idea of what's going on in the world of Imaro. What can you tell us, if anything, about – because I've been hearing rumours and whispers, something about *Rogues in the House* that – is there an Imaro t.v. series in the works? Do you know something about that?

M: There is – I guess I can say there's an effort to make it happen. There's another gentleman that Charles knew really well, his name is Taaq Kirksey. He met Taaq – well, actually, I think he met Taaq before I met him – and, Taaq was his – his charge was to get Imaro picked up in Hollywood. And it was something that he'd been working on for a long time. A few years ago, a producer got in contact with me, trying to find Charles and said he was interested in Imaro. And one thing lead to another and I got in con-

tact with Taaq and at this point – I don't think I'm spilling any beans right now because Taaq has talked about this – there is something that's in the works – I can't say where it is right now, at this point – but there is an effort being made to do that.

O: Well, I hope it goes all the way to the green light and gets out there because I think people will be ready for it.

M: Oh yeah, I think it would be great to see it. I mean, you know, it's something that really hasn't been done before. It's another reason why, that I started doing what I want to do because I look at these movies and I see people like Michael Clarke Duncan and folks like that and, like, these guys really need to have their own movies and shows in this same type of genre and stuff. A lot of times when I sat down and I was writing, I was thinking about these people and saying 'Hey, that would be great if they did this or they did that' kind of stuff. So, hopefully. There's been some things that kind of were delayed because of his passing. But, some things, as far as the estate is concerned, have been worked out. So, hopefully, we'll start seeing some things moving in that direction next year.

O: Well, that would be awesome because I'm – it almost feels cliché to say it at this point but – Black Panther made, like, a billion, right? Like, amongst all the things that have come out over the last few years. There's obviously an appetite that is not showing, you know, the more traditional faces we keep seeing in Spec Fic and Fantasy.

M: Exactly.

O: I would watch the hell out of that. Whether it's new stories or base it right off the first book.

I'm here for it. So, Marvel, if you're listening or whoever is producing... get this thing going. One of the things I've really liked about a lot of Sword & Soul stories – or the ones I've read. I don't want to pretend I've read everything – is the focus on a pre-colonial setting. Or, maybe I even just want to say they lack a European colonial aspect because, when applied to a different world than Earth, pre-colonial implies the colonial is 'inevitable?' Boy, would it be nice to remind ourselves that it isn't. So, I was very interested to see, like, just this morning as we're recording this, an article about your Changa's Safari series, which seems much closer to historical fiction or alt history than maybe the Sword & Soul I've seen so far. Because it includes colonial elements, it's rooted in our history – if I understand correctly – and even has some things in it like the slave trade. When you were coming up with Changa in the first place, what led you down this storytelling path rather than, say, a secondary world?

M: Well, Changa was my way to combine my two loves together: History and Fantasy. And, so, every book has a purpose, I guess, when I first started writing. When I wrote *Meji*, I wanted to write an epic fantasy that kind of expressed the size and the variety of cultures on the African continent. When I wrote *Changa's Safari*, I wanted to tell a good story for one, at first, but I also wanted to show the connections that Africa had with the rest of the world that a lot of people weren't aware of. Cause the Swahili culture were a sea-faring culture, a maritime culture, who were trading with East Asia as far as China. And I wanted to be able to show that. And that was part of the reason that I wrote *Changa's Safari*. Again, it allowed me to play in History like like I love and to

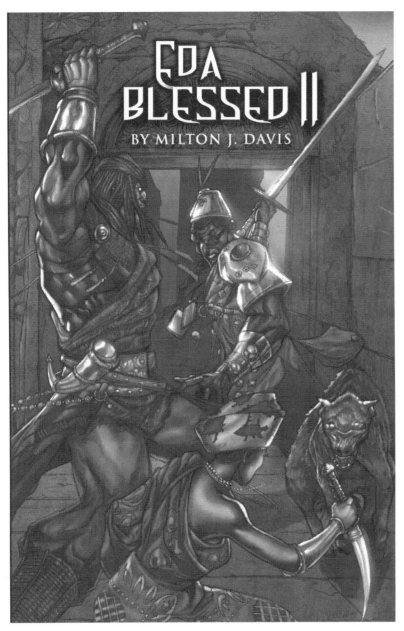

GOA BLESSED II

BY MILTON J. DAVIS

they [the Swahilis] were like 'Okay, Portuguese, cool. Whatchu got?' [*laughing*] You know? 'We've got ivory, we've got this, we've got that. Whatchu got?' You know, like 'What do you have to trade?' That kind of stuff like that. And I wanted to show that. I wanted to show that and express that in the books.

One of the most interesting things that happened after I released it was that a gentleman in Australia got in contact with me, after I released the first *Changa's Safari* book. And he said "I read the book. I had no idea about this history." And he went to research and he said, "You owned me up to something I didn't really realize, what was going on during that time." And to me, I want the books to be entertaining but I also like it when people read the books and learn something from it. Learn something about the culture.

O: That's a great explanation. I love it. Especially... well, there are five different directions I want to go in – that's so interesting. Okay, sorry – first up...

One thing that I was thinking of while you were saying that to me was, I often think of how, when Fritz Leiber was coming up with Lankmar and those guys, he was originally going to set it in antiquity era Alexandria. And then Lovecraft warned him, was like 'No, no, no. The history nerds are going to come for you. Make up your own place.' [*laughing*] And so, are you ready for the history nerds? Do you feel prepared for people being, like, 'Hang on. No, no, no. It was like this.'

M: Oh, they come for me and it's, in the most part it has been positive. People have read my stuff and they've actually said 'Hey, you know, I can tell that you've done your research.' And when they do have criticisms, it's like,

add that Fantasy element in it, too. And every place that Changa and his crew visits, I basically tried to reflect that region of the world the way it was in the fifteenth century. Not the world the way that we understand it now. And, so I had to do research into that, and I found out some very interesting things as I was doing it and understanding the myths and mythologies of those countries during that time period. So, it all kind of added to – to me, I felt it added to the richness of the story. And the entire time I was keeping people of African de-

scent in the forefront of the stories, the way that it would have been. You know, we talk about Marco Polo going to Asia and him writing about his stuff like that but the Swahili people were doing this on a daily basis. It was just part of life for them. When the Portuguese finally came around the cape and got to East Africa, they saw this thriving mercantile culture going on and it wasn't like, you know, sometimes you grow up in America, you keep thinking 'All these people weren't doing anything until Europeans arrived.' But, when you know, constructive criticism. Instead of them attacking what I said, they'll say 'Well, actually, this was kinda like this.' And the people that really get me – this is interesting, because I did a panel at Dragon-Con a couple of years ago, and we were talking about this. And I had a woman come up to me and she was like, "I can tell you did your research and I'm an archaeologist. You said sometime historians can be biased. If you want to get at the truth, read stuff by archaeologists. [laughing] Because we don't care about all that kind of stuff. We base what we say based on what we find."

So, it's been – you know you're going to miss some stuff. You're not going to get everything. And if you're not going to do it because you're afraid of getting something wrong, then you'll never do it. You know? You're going to get stuff wrong. I learned more about Swahili culture after I started writing Changa than when I was writing it. I was saying to myself, 'Man, I wish I had known this stuff when I first started writing the book. Cause I could have incorporated this and it would have made Changa's story more interesting.' A lot of the stuff I learned about Swahili culture that I didn't know before I started writing the book showed up in the prequel, before the Safari. Cause I went back and added that stuff in there. You're always learning something, so you can't not do it because you don't know everything, because part of the reason that you learned things is because you are doing it. And people are bringing you this additional information because you've started this journey and people are looking at what you're doing and they're saying 'Hey, I like this, but…' and then they'll get in contact with you and say 'Hey, check this out' or 'Research this,' that kind of thing.

O: Well, first of all, that archaeologist story, that must have been so gratifying. [laughing]

And, and as you say, you can always start moving the story forward or backward to add in the stuff that you've learned while working on it, right? Have you not come out with a volume of, essentially, origin stories for the Changa characters?

M: Well, actually, *Before the Safari* does do that. That's one of the things that I wanted to do in that book was, I actually give an origin story for each of the people – each of Changa's crew members. Major crew members. There's a story in there about Ponya, about the Toiree, about Prince Ackee, about Akele. And it shows, basically, what all of them were doing before they met Changa. What set them on their journey to meet Changa. And I also have an origin story about Changa in there. The first story is Changa's origin story. And it's mixed in with some other adventures that Changa takes part in before the actual Safari begins. That's why it's called *Before the Safari*, because all these little stories kind of lead you up to the beginning of the Safari. The last story is Prince Ackee's story which, if you've read the first book, it actually goes right up to the point where – just before Changa and the rest of his crew meet Prince Ackee.

O: I'm guessing people will probably want to start with the first book, not *Before* though, right?

M: The gentleman who wrote the article, Fletcher Vredenburgh, a big fan of Changa's - He said the *Before the Safari* book benefits more from having read the other books, before you read it. The first three books. I actually used it as a break before I wrote the final book in the series. I just went back and did *Before the Safari* – it gave me time to think about how

I was going to end the series, as I was writing that book. It kind of gave me a little break from telling the story.

O: I like that, too, because it's almost like going back and going 'Alright, before I get to this ending, let me really understand my characters.' Not that you didn't before, but to go even deeper.

M: Exactly. It was during that book that I was able to take a lot of the stuff that I had learned about the Swahili culture while I was writing the series and have it reflected in the last book – the final book of the Changa series, when I finally wrote it.

O: Well, I'm curious… I want to hear your take… A lot of Sword & Sorcery characters, you don't get origin stories – or, if you do, they come later. Like when Leiber stitched together his – you know, he wrote an origin story long after we were introduced to Fafhrd and Grey Mouser. How do you feel about the necessity and the proper timing, if you are going to tell it, of an origin story for your characters?

M: I think it depends on the story, the way you tell it. I always knew what Changa's origin was but I didn't really feel the need to tell it because I didn't feel like it was necessary to tell that origin. It was more of a – me doing it was more a response to people who started reading the books and were enjoying the books and they were asking those kind of questions. And when I decided to do *Before the Safari*, I said, I'm just going to start it off with Changa's origin. Because I already knew the story, so I'm just going to go ahead and tell it. I have another character, Omari Ket, who is – he comes from my Ki Khanga RPG world. And I started his series with his origin because, for him, who he is and what he ends up being has a lot to do with his origin and where he came from. So, that's why I started that story there because you needed to know what launched him into his life as an indentured mercenary. You know, what were the circumstances that started that. And that story also gives you a feel for the kind of person he is. It sets up who Omari Ket is. So, as you read the book, you know him as you go through the different adventures and that kind of thing.

O: Well, I think you've illustrated what my feeling is about this – and I'd like to hear if you agree. It seems like, origin stories, it's got be a conscious choice. It can't just be 'Well, you've gotta start at the beginning.' You know, I think that's where we get a lot of the lacklustre origin stories. Or the ones where people go back and write them because 'Well, I guess I gotta.' You know? I mean, like, *Ill Met in Lankhmar* is the one I always go to but the individual origin stories for Fafhrd and Grey Mouser – not great. Um… [*laughing*] And a lot of people tell you that. And I think it's just this thing that he's, you know, Leiber maybe felt like 'Aw, I've gotta go back and do this. I guess I'll do individual stories.' I mean, who knows, I haven't read his mind. But I feel like we've all seen that, the origin story that feels kind of… it's just there. You know?

M: Yeah. I mean, if you're going to do it - you have some people who just do it because maybe some agent came to them and said 'You need to write an origin story,' And to me, if it's not important, if it wasn't integral to the plot, the telling of the story, then why do it?

I'll bring this up as an example: like when I watch movies and stuff and they're written a certain way and then somebody says 'Hey, you know, we want to put in a black character' or something

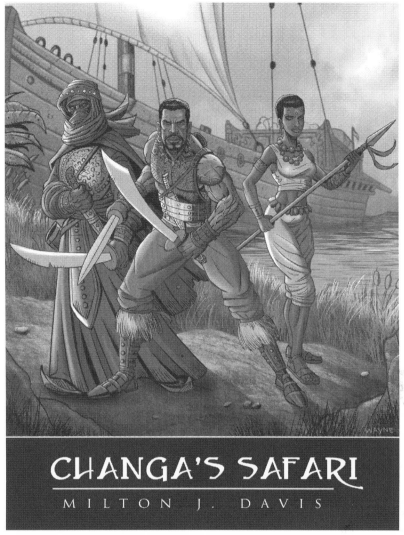

CHANGA'S SAFARI
MILTON J. DAVIS

like that and it's kind of an afterthought. And when they put the character in there it feels like it was an afterthought. It's as if somebody just tried to jam that into the story, you know? But when it's there in the beginning, it ties into the whole narrative as you see the whole story will improve. Whereas, like I said, when I went back to write Changa's origin story, it was not more of an add on or – any of the characters, really, because I already knew all their origin stories before I started writing *Changa's Safari*. So, I just wanted to start at a certain point in their life. I was just telling the stories that I already had figured out. And when you read the stories, you see how those stories connect to the personalities of the characters when

you met them, when the Safari started.

O: Yeah, and there was reader demand. You know, you'd already hooked people with the questions that came into their mind when they were reading these characters later in their lives.

M: I think it's really about – it's like, even when you look at Charles, I think it's about that background story being there in the beginning. Instead of somebody sitting down and saying, 'I'm going to write something like Conan.' And they start writing the stories and they never really have thought about the origin of these guys they just create the scenario and start writing it but there's no background that really explained where they came from.

O: Yeah, whereas like, with *Imaro*, it's noteworthy because you don't get to see a lot of Sword & Soul or Sword & Sorcery heroes who start as children. You get a little bit of him as a kid and boy, is it integral – I won't spoil it for the listener. But trust me, it's there for a good reason.

M: Exactly.

O: But then meanwhile, while you were talking there it kept making me think of – have you ever seen a movie that is like, the title is 'Such and Such: Origins' and you're excited? Whenever I've seen that, I'm like, 'Aw, man. No, this is not going to be good.'

M: And it's usually somebody going back that, the stories have been told, and they say 'Hey, you know what? I want to do – we want to tell how this stuff all started'. And they weren't the people that basically created the story or had a feel for the story, so, they really weren't in the author's mind on what they were thinking about when they wrote it. And it shows when you get this origin story.

O: Yeah. And you're like 'And that's where he got his pants from. Okay, sure.' Usually it's not even answering any of the big questions. Alright, okay.

M: I'm not going to say the series but there was somebody who did – there was a prequel series done from a series that I really like. And one of the worst prequel books was almost like that. The book was written just to explain one aspect of the story. And it ended so abruptly, I'm like, 'So, why even write this?' It had nothing to do with everything else that what was going on in the novel. It was almost like, I just want to explain this, I'm going to write this

few chapters just to explain that, and then I'm just going to leave it alone.

O: Yeah, and maybe also make a few dollars off of a franchise somebody else built. But maybe that's cynical of me. I don't know. Anyway, I could rag on this all day. [*laughing*] Listen, you mentioned it, I really want to get into it.

And MV Media isn't just doing books and comics – the table-top role playing game with Ki Khanga, could you tell the people a little bit about that? And about your personal connection to the table-top RPG hobby? Were you playing D&D in the basement when you were, like, eleven? Or, is it a new thing? How did this all come about for you?

M: Okay, true confession. Like a friend of mine says, "Confession is good for the soul but bad for the reputation." [*laughing*] I had never played an RPG game before we created Ki Khanga.

O: Oh, dear. [*laughing*]

M: I'm just going to go ahead and lay that out there. The reason it happened was because my creative partner, Bal, has played RPG games for forty or fifty years. He has played them for a long time. And when he was playing the games, he'd started off with Dungeons & Dragons and, like most black people playing a game, he noticed this lack of representation. So, he would create his own scenarios for his D&D friends. And he would incorporate African culture into it. Not too long after we met, he and I were having a discussion and we started talking about that. Him and I are the kind of people, the reason we get along so well, we see stuff like that and we say, 'Okay, let's do it.' Instead of just complaining about it, we said, "Okay, let's do it." So, we were

talking about this and, I guess it was serendipity or whatever, we were getting ready to do a presentation and there were a number of people on the panel. And as we were talking about it, this one guy came over to us and said "Are you guys talking about RPGs?" And we said, "Yeah." And he said, "My name is Ed Hall." And then Bal's eyes got big and he said, "You're THE Ed Hall?" And I'm sitting there dumbfounded, like, what's this Ed Hall guy? And he [B] says, "This guy is like an editor for White Wolf. He's done this game and he's done that game." So, all three of us started talking. And we talked about the idea we were thinking about and he said, "Hey, well, you know, you guys get it together and let me know and I'll take a look at it and give you guys some pointers, or something like that." So, that's how that all came to be.

And my involvement in Ki Khanga was more creating the back stories and developing the world. Whereas Bal... 's main point is he's basically the game master, he's our Griot. He's the one that created the playing system, the different levels, and all those kind of details. And then we wrote it out a few years ago. It was different than most RPG games because we based it on a card playing system, as opposed to dice. We're actually working right now on Ki Khanga 2.0 which is going to incorporate dice because, you know, we got tired of people crying about it. [*laughing*] There were some people that really jumped onto the card thing and there were others who were like, ' I want more dice.' So, *2.0*, which is going to come out and it's going to have a dice playing system incorporated into it.

But that's where that all came about. Again, it was Sword & Soul. We developed the anthology because we wanted to give people ideas about how to create the adventures. And by telling these different stories and stuff, we were trying to give everybody ideas. Because we know a lot of people aren't familiar with African culture, so, they're trying to figure out, 'How do I tell the story this way?' And so we said, 'Well, we're going to give you some examples. And then maybe from these examples you can go on and create some of your own adventures.'

O: And, well, parallel to that, I saw you're Sword & Soul World-building video. Which, I thought was pretty solid.

So, yeah, it's kind of cool actually, to see another pre-colonial game out there. Have you heard of Coyote and Crow?

M: I have not heard of that.

O: Okay. You might want to check it out, just out of curiosity. It is a pre-colonial North American indigenous peoples RPG.

M: Oh yeah, I did hear about that. I did see that. 'Cause I know, as far as African-based, it was a game back in the day called Nyumbai - or something like that – that was out and it was funny because, as we were doing ours, we found out that a lot of times things that we'd do would end up influencing other people.

O: For the listener, 'influencing' was put in quotation marks. So, that's interesting. I mean, stealing is flattery, I guess? I don't know. [*laughing*]

M: Yeah, sometimes I know. We talk about it sometimes but, well, we had a particular character in Ki Khanga called the Frog Hag, and there was a story behind her. And, not too long after the game came out, a particular well known RPG company came out with a character that – the illustration of the character looked exactly like our Frog Hag.

O: And it was, like, the Toad Witch. [*laughing*]

M: Something like that. And even worse than that, I recently saw some person – they came out with – they were a smaller company - not only did the copy the character Kidera from Ki Khanga, they used the same name. They called their character Kidera.

O: Oh, boy. It's like, make an effort. I mean, I know you're copying but... [*laughing*]

M: Yes, it was – it's been an interesting journey. But, you know, like they say 'Imitation is the sincerest form of flattery.' I guess we should be flattered by this. [*laughing*]

O: I guess. I mean – okay, well, let's encourage people to get the original. The original flavour.

Speaking of being ready for the nerds to come for you, I hope your RPG buddies have warned you. When you come out with a second edition, that's going to start the 'edition wars.' You're going to have people being like, 'No, first edition's better. Cards, man, you've gotta use the cards!'

M: It was interesting, when we first rolled the game out because we did test playing and we picked different groups of people [who] would test the game out and see what they think about it – and it was distinct differences. Some of the old D&D veterans started complaining right off the bat, saying 'You guys don't have categories. Like, wizard and warrior and stuff like that. You're not using the dice. And blah, blah blah.' And we're like, okay, because this is not Dungeons & Dragons. [*laughing*]

O: 'I don't like this. You made your own thing.' [*laughing*]

M: Yeah, this is not D&D. But then we had people who had never played role playing games before that we introduced it to and they liked it. They liked the card system. They had no prior experience. Then we had – I hate to say it, it's an age based thing – then we had younger people that played Dungeons and Dragons and then came Ki Khanga and they enjoyed it. They got right into the differences and stuff like that. I found out that the role playing game community, the players are very loyal to whatever they've been playing. Because some of them have been playing it for decades... with the same people... in the same character. And so, we're never trying to convert people. We're not trying to get somebody to stop playing this and play that. What we're trying to do is just create our own game and find people that are interested in it. And when people get very upset, I just tell them, well, basically, 'This is a game. We're not trying to convert you. We're not trying to be Dungeons & Dragons. We're creating our own game. Either you're going to look at it and be interested and play it and enjoy it... or you're not.'

O: I always find it funny when people get like that. Like, what, you can't enjoy two games? You just eat one food?

M: Exactly.

Yeah, I'll tell you one interesting note, though. I was very surprised by the interest we got in Brazil. We had a lot of people in Brazil that really loved Ki Khanga - So much so, that we had one company that wanted to make a Brazilian version of the game. They wanted to bring it in and do it in Brazilian Portuguese. At the time we were being very cautious about exposing the game because we were concerned about people, you know, taking it and trying to do their own things and

Ki Khanga
SWORD & SOUL ROLE PLAYING GAME
BASIC RULES

BY
**Balogun
Ojetade &
Milton
Davis**

stuff like that. But it's something that we're revisiting now because we're seeing a lot of interest in other countries like that and having a version of the game where the language has been translated to something that they would make it easier for people in different countries is something we're starting to focus on and look at now.

O: I don't count as an expert but I've been an avid hobbyist for decades and, like, as far as I know, there is a very strong role playing game scene down there. And Germany, too. I remember every game I got into – I was a big *Shadowrun* fan, I don't know if you've ever heard of that one, it's like cyberpunk meets magic. And I

just remember being stunned that they had German translations of all their books. Like, 'You do that over there?' I'm just some dumb kid growing up... There's definitely markets outside of the ones you'd expect.

As far as the older players, I hear you. It sounds like you did the smart thing any businessman does, you found the talent to bring in to handle the stuff you're unfamiliar with, the game mechanics, that kind of thing. So, I'm just curious, though – have you come across or encountered the term 'Grognard?'

M: No, I haven't.

O: It's like an oldish term unto itself. I forget exactly when it was

coined. It basically – it originally was the term for the oldest soldiers in Napoleon's army who would always kind of bitch and complain about things. They're like, 'Well, we've been around. We can do whatever, right?' And that term ended up – you know, because D&D came out of war gaming, that term got grafted onto the older, more curmudgeonly players who were like, 'Argh, a card system in a role playing game?!?' So, yeah, maybe next time someone gives you that grief you can be like, 'Hey man, I don't listen to grognards.' [*laughing*]

M: Well, that's a term I'll have to keep in mind.

Yeah, I mean, Ki Khanga was the first role playing game that I ever played. As we played, I was – I could see why people would be interested and why people play role playing games. Because you're basically creating the story as you go.

O: Yeah, I love it. I love the clever story telling and you get these – you know, I'm still having laughs from games I played, like, fifteen years ago with the same buddies. You remember it just as much as like a crazy party story, or whatever.

M: Yeah, and there's a number of gamemasters who have become novel writers because they're basically story tellers.

O: Yeah, back and forth, people move along that axis, for sure. I could talk about that all day long but let's move on. It's one of my favourite hobbies. I'm getting my old group back tomorrow for the first time since COVID but, um, this is not about me. Let's move on, Oliver. You can tell I'm an only child, right?

So, Sword & Soul isn't just writing and gaming, as we were just discussing. It's also some pretty cool artwork. And you're adapting *Changa's Safari* into comic books. And last September, in your interview with *Indie Comics Dispatch*, that you said you guys – MVmedia – are going to be getting further into comics, wanting to get into animation, as well. I mean, that could be an hour unto itself. But, maybe briefly, who are some of your favourite artists that you've worked with? What style do you feel works best for the genre?

M: That's a tough question. Because I love all the artists I work with. I choose them based on what I think they bring to the story. I grew up around my cousins – I had two cousins who were artists. Unfortunately, I didn't have the talent. They let me know that very early on. [*laughing*] But I've always been surrounded by it. So, when I started developing these stories and these characters – I used to be part of a group called 'Black Superhero.' And it was basically a forum of black comic book artists and I got a lot of these guys' works and a lot of them are people I work with now because I became familiar with their artwork in this group. It was a very volatile group but I'd always pull people aside and say, "Hey, I really like your artwork. Can you do this for me? Can you do that for me?"

I think I could talk about it more along the lines of people I've worked with the longest. One particular artist would be Stanley Weaver Jr. I've been working with Stanley probably almost as long as I've been publishing. And when we first started working together, Stan was more of a contemporary comic book, futuristic-type artist and he didn't really have a lot of background on the regions and the cultures that I was looking at. So, I would send him photographic references and he was very good at looking at

those references and coming up with something for me. At this point now, he's real easy for me to work with because he knows me and I know him and all I have to do is say, 'Hey Stan, I'm working on this new Omari Ket novel, this is what I'm looking for.' I may send him a couple of references. And then he comes back and – BAM – he hit's it out of the park. He has a dynamic style and his artwork is very energetic, has a lot of motion in it. And sometimes that's what I'm looking for when I'm doing a particular story.

Other artists that I work with – one artist that you have to talk about is Mashindo Kumba. Mashindo is phenomenal. If you've seen the more recent Imaro books, Mashindo is the person that's done the cover for those.

O: Oh, yeah yeah, three and four in particular I'm thinking of.

M: That's his artwork. He did the cover for our Ki Khanga anthology, my Ki Khanga game, that's – he's done that work. He's a person that – artist that's into the Afrocentric vibe. So, he's another one that's very easy to work with when it comes to that. We've done some work with Bryan Syme. Brian does a lot of RPG illustrations. Actually, when we started Ki Khanga, he got in contact with us and said, "Hey, I think this is a great idea. I'd love to do some artwork for you guys." So, that's how we worked with him. There's so many of them – like I said, I love them all. I really can say. Shakira Rivers , a young lady that's out of Florida, I worked with her. She did the cover for *Priestess of nKu* and I've known her for a long time. I love her style of artwork. She did some artwork that I used for *Before the Safari*. Again, each of them brings – they bring their own flavour to it. That's why I don't use them on every project but there's certain

projects when I pull up I say, "Hey, I know this is perfect for Shakira. This is a great one for Stan." That kind of thing.

I probably answered your question without answering it. [*laughing*]

O: No no no, that's all good. I just wanted your thoughts and things and it sounds, definitely, you've got me – I noticed there was a very comic book feel to a lot of the art. That's why.

M: That's why. A lot of my artists are comic book artists. You get that vibe from them, which is okay with me. I like that. You have somebody like, for instance, Edison Moody, he did the cover to *The City*. Edison is more what you would see, your more traditional cover art type artist. And it reflects on that when you see the cover of that book.

So, it's a lot of different artists.

O: I think we almost kind of illustrated with this question - but I often wrap up interviews with things along the lines of, you know, who would recommend, whatever. But there's always this fear in the guest where they're like, 'Ah, I don't want to forget Bob. I love Bob.' Or whoever. So, it's kind of anxiety inducing. But I'm trying to get better. Let's see if I've gotten better.

What I would instead like to ask, which is maybe more of an appropriate question of you in your publishing role, who is the latest author you've taken on board – how did that go, what made you decide that they were worth investing in?

M: There's three authors that I've currently published, each of them for different reasons.
When it comes to Sword & Soul, there's an author called Sarah Macklin. And Sarah we published – the first thing I published by

Sarah was her story in our *Griot: Sisters of the Spear*. As a matter of fact, her story is the opening story for the book. Because I was so impressed by it. When I read it, I was like, 'This is a great story.' And we published a book by her recently called *The Royal Heretic*. That is one of the best Sword & Soul, Sword & Sorcery, epic fantasy stories I've ever read. I was blown away by it when I read it because I was like, this is her first book and she just nails everything. She's created such a foundation – and I'm glad this is going to be a series. It was a kind of book that I read that, when I first, when I ended, I was like, 'Okay, what's the second part?' [*laughing*] I gotta see where this story is going to go.

Another author that I published recently is a brother by the name of Enoch Zembaya. Enoch's actually from Zambia. He got in contact with me, he said he read *Griot: Sisters of the Spear* and he was inspired by it and he sent me a story that became a novel. I like him because he has a very epic fantasy feel to his work. And he's working from an indigenous African culture. So, that brings a perspective to the story telling that's something that Charles and I talked about. Because initially, most Sword & Soul was coming from African American authors and them doing their research. We always talked about, 'I wonder how this story telling is going to be when we start getting authors from African cultures?' and Enoch is one of those. And there's a lot of them out there now and they're telling some great stories.

There's also B. Sharice Moore whose book I just published, *Dr. Marvellus Djinn's Odd Scholars*, which is a – which goes into my steam punk/diesel punk genres. And, again, anther great storyteller. I read a great book by her years ago and she does a really good job of incorporating

history and fiction and just putting it all together to make a great book. Actually, we released it this year and it was our best performing release ever. I was kind of envious because she sold more books than I've sold of my own. [*laughing*]

O: Another publisher/writer problem.

M: Yeah, exactly.

O: It's like, I'm happy as a publisher. As a writer...

M: "Why are they outselling me ?!?" [*laughing*] But it's a good problem to have.

O: I've really enjoyed chatting with you. I've got, like, thirty more questions – maybe we should do this again some time.

M: I'm available.

O: Let's get into the final question: What are you and MVmedia working on now? Like, what's the newest stuff people can check out or in the new future? And where can people find you?

M: We've got a number of books coming out that have actually been released this year. They're basically paperback versions of books that we had in e-book fashion. Like *Fallen*, which is a Sword & Soul series based in the Changa

universe. It's out right now. We have another one coming out called *The Long Walk*, which is a steamfunk story. It's a really interesting story. I think people would enjoy it.

I'm actually – one of the things that I like is that I get to work with authors that I admire and so, this year we actually have a – we're releasing a – re-releasing a book by an author Minister Faust called *The Alchemist of Kush*. I actually read the book years ago and loved it and I met Minister Faust a few years ago when he came to Atlanta to speak at Georgia Tech and so we developed a relationship. And I was like, "Hey man, I really would like to publish a book by you." He said, "Hey, great. How about *The Alchemist of Kush*?" And I was like, "Ah, man – I get to publish my favourite book by you?!" It's a great book. Minister Faust is a great story teller. I've published some of his short stories in some of my anthologies.

So, those are probably the main books that we're working on right now.

I've got a serial novel that's going to be on my Patreon called *Black Rose*, which is actually my first historical fiction novel. Again, I go to the Swahili culture but this is a book about a Swahili merchant who ends up taking in a Japanese princess on the request of her father because their family is under dire situation. So, I talk about this relationship between them and how she ends up actually eventually taking this young girl to East Africa and raising her within the Swahili culture. So, I'm really excited about that one. That one will be coming out, as well. That's going to be an MVmedia Patreon launching next month. And I'm going to have certain stories that are going to be specific to the Patreon that, after they become full fledged novels and I release them, but to read them as we're developing

them, if you're a Patreon member you can follow them as we...

O: Oh, very cool! Also you're further utilizing that you're both author and publisher.

I was just in my last interview talking with someone about how you see some author's releasing early drafts of their chapters on their Patreon but then they try and get it published and they run into trouble. You kind of already put this out, so...

M: Well, you know, because I'm the publisher. [*laughing*]

O: Exactly. No problem!

M: *No* problem with that!

We also have a couple of animation projects we're working on. One called *Playing the Odds*, which is a CyberFunk series that we're working on right now. We've got a great team working together on that. We've got the *From Here to Timbuktu* animation that I'm working on with Avaloy Studios in Atlanta. We've got a pilot out – we're actually working on getting that done, as well. We'll probably be announcing crowd funders for both of those projects in the near future. To get them going.

Lot of stuff going on.

O: Very cool. Awesome. Well, like I said, I could just chat with you all day. And if you're ever up in Toronto, I'll buy you a beer. But right here, right now, I guess I should tie it off. Again, thank you so much for being here, Milton.

M: Thanks for having me, man. Enjoyed it.

Oliver Brackenbury grew up around the corner from a five story deep cold war bunker, as one does, and can now be found living not far from a popular 1,815.4 ft tower in Toronto.

He mostly writes novels and screenplays, in a variety of genres, hosts the *So I'm Writing a Novel...* and *Unknown Worlds of the Merril Collection* podcasts, and edits this very magazine. Heck, he'll even edit your writing, if you pay him! He loves to talk story.

oliverbrackenbury.com
@obracken

Interview transcribed by Tania Morrison

The Outsider in Sword & Sorcery

Brian Murphy

Sword & Sorcery has sharp edges. It is the literature of disunion and revolt, of rage against the machine. The aggrieved, the disenfranchised, are its protagonists. We know them as the outsider.

Practically all the iconic figures of Sword & Sorcery are outsiders. Kull, exile of Atlantis, is an unwelcome barbarian on the throne of civilized Valusia, many on his court ceaselessly plotting his destruction. Karl Edward Wagner's Kane is a wandering outcast, a tormented loner who finds solace in a series of shallow encounters with women. Ageless, he is unable to die from means other than violence and so remains alienated from society. Michael Moorcock's Elric, though a member of the ruling class of Melnibonéans, is uneasy in his own skin, sick with the depravities inflicted by his dwindling, corrupt race. Fritz Leiber's Fafhrd and the Gray Mouser listen to the celebrations of nobles from the cold, empty streets of Lankhmar—and they like it that way. "We go our own way, choosing our own adventures—and our own follies! Better freedom and a chilly road than a warm hearth and servitude."

Charles Saunders's Imaro is another memorable outsider. His mysterious origins lie outside the fierce, proud, and insular group of warriors known as the Ilyassai. Bullied mercilessly as a youth, Imaro reaches prodigious size and strength as a young man, but his physical gifts intimidate his peers. Consumed by loneliness, Imaro experiences freedom only when walking alone among the tall grasses of the Tamburure, where he sees himself reflected in the lion. "It was then that he felt he belonged in the Tamburure, at one with the vast herds of impala, zebra, kudu, gazelle, and countless other creatures that roamed where there will guided them. Even more did the youth identify with the predators."

These aren't (usually) heroes fighting for the established order. Think hall-wreckers, mead-drinkers. Marginalized victims who have had enough and stand up and strike back against their oppressors. Often that leads them on a lonely road. But they like it that way.

Whether it features a badass female swordslinger who knocks the teeth out of grasping men or a bare-chested barbarian who ransacks the palace court and carves a blood-soaked path to the very throne itself, Sword & Sorcery and its outsider heroes subvert our expectations.

Robert E. Howard did not invent the idea of the noble savage, but his application of this concept to fantasy was revolutionary.

Conan is something very different than the noble knights of King Arthur's court or even the folk hero Robin Hood, who robbed from the rich, but out of altruism. He is a barbarian, wild, often out for himself, but possessed of a moral code, as contrasted with the decadence and decay inherent in civilized society. This made the subgenre rather transgressive when Howard gave it birth in the pages of *Weird Tales*. It remained so when Moorcock and Leiber conspired to give it a name, and new outsiders, in the pages of the fanzine *Amra* in the 1960s.

Many of the authors, artists, and visionaries of Sword & Sorcery were themselves outsiders. Howard is our chief example. An intellectual who recoiled at working routine day jobs for the man and turned to writing for the pulps, Howard lived in a time and place (1920s/30s rural Texas) ill-fitted to his vocation and skeptical of his eccentric ways. Monstrously talented painter Jeffrey Catherine Jones (multiple Hugo nominee, winner of the World Fantasy Award for Best Artist in 1986) and shrewd, incisive author and editor Jessica Amanda Salmonson (World Fantasy Award winner for 1979's *Amazons!*), both trans, were very much outsiders in their day and age, challenging the status quo of the time with their very humanity.

At its best, Sword & Sorcery remains transgressive today even as it changes and adapts, as it must, for modern times and new audiences.

There is plenty of room for creativity within its template. "Outsider" needn't be synonymous with "barbarian," the cliched fur-diapered, horned-helmeted warrior of the northern wastes. Barbarians became so comically ubiquitous in the Sword & Sorcery of the 1970s and 80s that they fell to self-parody, mocked by Sword & Sorcery author Poul Anderson in the likes of "On Thud and Blunder." The word barbarian derives from the ancient Greek *barbaros*, a term applied to anyone not a citizen of Greece speaking in a foreign tongue. In short, a barbarian is anyone from the outside, the wild, uncivilized places of the world. The places where Sword & Sorcery heroes dwell.

Because it is the literature of the outsider, Sword & Sorcery offers a rich vicarious experience for the reader. We can share headspace with the likes of Jirel of Joiry, who plunges into a literal and symbolic underworld in "Black God's Kiss," representative of the struggles of a woman in a male-dominated world, an outsider even though she's a lord. This is a Good Thing. In this age of curated online spaces where we can filter out opposing opinions and anyone who is not like us, Sword & Sorcery broadens our experiences of the world and opens up the richness within it.

But beware, Sword & Sorcery is unpredictable.

Sometimes its edge cuts in ways you may approve. When Kull smashes the stone tablets of a stifling, backwards, corrupt empire that refuses to recognize a marriage between two love-smitten youths of different castes, and creates new law, we pump our fist. *"By this axe I rule!"* If only change were so easy.

But the blade can turn and cut the hand that wields it. In the pages of Sword & Sorcery you will encounter morally gray, semi-likeable jerks like Cugel the Clever, or utterly amoral, irredeemable bastards like Liane the Wayfarer, who have their way with unwary, too-trusting travelers. Half the characters in the stories of Clark Ashton Smith are not folks you would want to hang out with.

But they are nevertheless great, because they are different, and give us visions into wildness, dark places of the world, and the wide expressions of the human soul.

If you place guardrails on that freedom, you've bled the subgenre of the vitality that gives it its unique character. If you can tolerate the discomfort, you might understand why a story need be told as it is. Great art contains dangerous visions.

This is how it should be, and needs to be, if the genre is to continue to thrive and grow. After a period of dormancy and near life support, Sword & Sorcery has shown modest signs of a comeback.

Let's not choke it out in the cradle. It won't survive with sameness and conformity. We need diversity in the true richness and complexity of what that word really means. We don't need culling or excision, we need a broad tent that welcomes all outsiders, inside.

We don't need a dulled blade. We need a New Edge that's sharp and can cut, both ways.

Welcome, outsider, from whatever byways you roam.

Brian Murphy is the author of *Flame and Crimson: A History of Sword-and-Sorcery* (Pulp Hero Press, 2020). Learn more about his life and work on his website, The Silver Key.

thesilverkey.blogspot.com

Gender Performativity in Howard's "Sword Woman"

Nicole Emmelhainz

Robert E. Howard's character Dark Agnes demonstrates the flexibility characters have within the Sword & Sorcery genre to push the boundaries of their genders and reimagine what performance of gender might look like. Howard, the prolific pulp writer, is considered one of the founding authors of weird fiction and Sword & Sorcery, with his Conan the Cimmerian being the most recognizable today. And though many of the notable Sword & Sorcery characters are men, including Fritz Leiber's Fafhrd and the Grey Mouser, Michael Moorcock's Elric of Melniboné, and Karl Edward Wagner's Kane, there are notable women characters including C.L. Moore's Jirel of Joiry and C.J. Cherryh's Morgaine. With Dark Agnes, Howard created a female character – a Sword Woman – who helped define female protagonists within the weird fiction and by extension, the Sword & Sorcery genre, by challenging traditional feminine gender performances. Over the course of the three-story sequence — "Sword Woman," "Blades for France," and the incomplete "Mistress of Death" — Howard creates a space in which Agnes can test the limits of her gender performance, and where the option for a third gender becomes available to the character: she is not man nor a woman but another kind of gendered character entirely.

In the opening of "Sword Woman," Agnes de Chastillon appears confined by the expectations not only of her cruel father but also her gender. Forced to marry, in her words, a "munching, guzzling, nuzzling swine" (332) named Francois who her father believes will help him maintain their land and "tame" her as

well, the future looks bleak for Agnes. As she awaits the wedding ceremony, she sits in the family's hut, in wedding finery that "was more loathsome than the slimy touch of a serpent," feeling as though she's "caught in a trap in which [she] struggled in vain" (332-333). But when her sister slips her a dagger, with the implication that Agnes should end her own life, rather than feel her body "grow bent [..] and broken with child bearing" and her mind "grow strange and grey — with the toil and the weariness — and the everlasting face of a man [she] hates," something changes for Agnes. No longer does she have just two choices: to either marry and allow the expectations of her sex and gender to destroy her or to kill herself. With the touch of the blade in her hand, a third choice opens to her. Though Agnes does not yet have the capacity to articulate what she's feeling that dagger contains a "strange sense of familiarity;" it is, in her words, "like an old friend come home again" (334).

Gender, according to theorist Judith Butler, is a concept unique to every individual, and comes into being through a series of repeated performances. Butler believes that bodily and nonverbal cues specifically structure gender. This understanding of gender centers on notions of performances, which can take on different forms throughout a person's life. As Butler explains, gender is "a stylized repetition of acts [...] which are internally discontinuous [...] [so that] the appearance of substance is precisely that, a *constructed identity*, a performative accomplishment which the mundane social audience, including the actors themselves, come to believe and to perform in the mode of belief" (179, emphasis

mine). In other words, gender is not simply a consequence of being alive and being born into a particular biological sex, but is a constantly changing series of choices an individual makes over a lifetime.

Howard's characterization of Dark Agnes provides a lens through which to understand "constructed identity." Most protagonists associated with the weird fiction and Sword & Sorcery genres are male, masculine-focused characters that often act in exaggerated fashion, their fighting, drinking, and lustful desires playing out repeatedly through embodied performances, usually to an awestruck crowd of onlookers as well as the readers. But the same can be argued about the women protagonists present within the genres. In Agnes's origin story "Sword Woman," the transformation the protagonist makes is marked through several key moments in the narrative. These moments highlight the choices she makes in bringing about her preferred gendered identity.

Much of Agnes's experience throughout this first story centers on her body and its physicality. Agnes's sister describes her as having a "tall, supple" body (333). When she first encounters Etienne Villiers after her flight from the village of la Fere, he describes her in this way: "By Saint Trignan, you fit a high and noble name better than many high born ladies I have seen simpering and languishing under it. Zeus and Apollo, but you are a tall lithe wench" (337). In fact, despite Etienne's attempt to disguise her in men's clothing, Agnes's physical feminine features are difficult to hide: "The blindest clod in the fields could tell 'twas no man those garments hid" (338). Agnes, though, seems not bothered by others' reactions to and comments about her overtly female body.

She often uses moments like this to reassert her decisions regarding her gendered performance. In "Blades for France," when Agnes comes across a stranger she later learns was the hired killer La Balafre, she exclaims the following when he tries to force himself on her: "Fool! [...] Must I slay half the men in France to teach them respect? Look ye! I wear these garments but as the garb and tools of my trade, not to catch the attention of men. I drink, fight and live like a man --" (366). Here, Agnes demonstrates she is in charge of the way in which she experiences the world and the way in which she wants others to understand her. Though she has physical features of a woman that cannot be concealed through clothing or the chopping off of her red hair, the way in which she carries herself and interacts with others — both men and women — show she is not merely a woman pretending to be a man, but something else entirely.

References to physical sensations felt in or through her body also shape the narrative and frame the manner in which her transformation takes place. Throughout the beginning of "Sword Woman," a time in which Agnes still thinks of herself as a "girl," much of her experience is described through detailed sensory imagery. For example, when her father reiterates that Agnes's fiancé will be able to tame her, her response is visceral: "At that a red mist waved across my sight. It was ever thus at such talk of taming. [...] all the fire in my blood rushed to my lips" (332). The visual description of the "red mist" before her eyes along with the physical feeling of blood rushing to her lips show that Agnes's sensory acuity guides her

actions. The implied backstory of her father trying to tame her suggests that throughout her life, Agnes has challenged the expectations placed on her by being categorized as woman, often met with physical abuse. To this point, her life has been defined not by how she wants it, but by these forced expectations. Yet there appears something innate that will allow her to better realize the life she wants, including the performed gender she desires, once she escapes these expectations.

The first part of her transformation occurs when she faces her fiancé Francois during her wedding ceremony: "At the sight of him I ceased my struggles like one stuck motionless [...] so I stood facing him for an instant, almost crouching, glaring unspeaking. 'Kiss her, lad!' bellowed some drunken lout; and then as a taut spring snaps, I jerked the dagger from my bosom and sprang at Francois. My act was too quick for those slow witted clowns to even comprehend, much less prevent. My dagger was sheathed in his pig's heart before he realized I had struck, and I yelped with mad glee to see the stupid expression of incredulous surprize and pain his flood red countenance" (334). Several details highlight Agnes's realization of agency in her ability to now act in the way that's truer to her preferred gender expression: at first, much like the girl in the woods momentarily was, she's dumbstruck and frozen by the situation she's been placed in by these men. However, with the dagger — which has previously stirred in her "a dim train of associations [she] could not understand but somehow felt" (334) — she is able to act in surprising ways that allow her to take control of the situation. This includes when she learns of Etienne's plan to sell her to Thibault and when Tristan's gang comes to kill Etienne for his assumed

killing of Thibault. Howard's narrative suggests when Agnes is able to allow her innate sensibilities to direct her actions and life, she is not only able to get the better of men who would try to force her back into a prescribed gender performance she does not want, but can then assert her desires to live her life through a certain kind of performance that enacts her true gendered self.

The transformation Agnes experiences after she kills her would-be husband and flees from her abusive father becomes complete in a scene of rebirth. After spending the night in the forest, Agnes awakes at dawn: "it found me alive and whole, and possessed of a ravenous hunger. I sat up, wondering for an instant at the strangeness of it all, then the sight of my torn wedding robes and the blood-crusted dagger in my girdle brought it all back. I laughed again as I remembered Francois' expression as he fell, and a wild surge of freedom flooded me, so I felt like dancing and singing like a mad woman. But instead I cleansed the dagger on some fresh leaves, and putting it again in my girdle, I went toward the rising sun" (335). She recognizes that she is now a "whole" person, having removed herself from the confines of the village and the men who wished to define her life. Her "ravenous hunger" also suggests she will now be able to take pleasure in life and better enjoy the physicality of her body. Finally, Agnes makes a decision not to dance and sing like a mad woman, but instead clean off her dagger and move on, with apparent new focus found only through enacting a gender expression that presents herself as who she wants to be.

Though there are additional key passages that demonstrate Agnes's transformation and achievement of her preferred gender, I want to close with this long passage from the exchange

Agnes has with Guiscard de Clisson. When she asks to ride with him into battle in Italy because she is "weary of being a woman," de Clisson laughs at her. Though he initially asks her if she is a man or woman, he only sees a woman in men's clothing. Agnes, however, declares that there is more in her than what she outwardly appears:

Ever the man in men! Let a woman know her proper place: let her milk and spin and sew and bake and bear children, nor look beyond her threshold or the command of her lord and master! Bah! I spit on you all! There is no man alive who can face me with weapons and live, and before I die, I'll prove it to the world. Women! Cows! Slaves! Whimpering, cringing serfs, crouching to blows, revenging themselves by — taking their own lives, as my sister urged me to do. Ha! You deny me a place among men? By God, I'll live as I please and die as God wills, but if I'm not fit to be a man's comrade, at least I'll be no man's mistress. (350)

In this last declaration, she makes clear her intention: to live not as either a man or a woman. Though Howard continues to use these gender markers to describe Agnes throughout all three stories, I believe that Agnes is neither. She asserts her gender performance as something beyond the common identifiers of man and woman, something of a third gender. Moving beyond the expectations of both men and women allows the character of Agnes to finally experience her life the way she knew it should always be: "I seemed to have been born into a new world, and yet a world for which I was intended from birth. My former life seemed like a dream, soon to be forgotten" (355).

Weird fiction, and certainly Sword & Sorcery, writers today can look back to pulp writers like Howard for ways to explore gen-der, sexuality, and identity in representative and compelling ways. The genre accommodates and invites such explorations.

Works Cited

Butler, Judith. *Gender Trouble*. Routledge: New York, 1990.

Howard, Robert E. *The Coming of Conan the Cimmerian*. Del Rey: New York, 2003.

———. *Sword Woman and Other Historical Adventures*. Del Rey: New York, 2011.

Nicole Emmelhainz is Associate Professor of Composition and Rhetoric at Christopher Newport University, where she also directs the Alice F. Randall Writing Center and serves as Writing Program Administer. She received her MA in English from Ball State University, her MA in Creative Writing Poetry from Ohio University, and her PhD in Writing History and Theory from Case Western Reserve University. She is the co-editor for *The Dark Man: Journal of Robert E. Howard and Pulp Studies* and has presented widely on elements of pulp fiction, sword and sorcery, and feminism.

The Obanaax: And Other Tales of Heroes and Horrors
Review by Robin Marx

When Kirk A. Johnson encountered fantasy, it was love at first sight. The introduction to *The Obanaax: And Other Tales of Heroes and Horrors*, Johnson's self-published debut collection, describes how as a child he was instantly transfixed by the Rankin/Bass animated adaptation of *The Hobbit*. Subsequent exposure to the 1950s Hercules movies and the stop-motion classics by Ray Harryhausen deepened his enthusiasm for the genre. He devoured comics like *Conan the Barbarian* and *Warlord* before moving on to more foundational works of fantasy, such as those by Robert E. Howard and the Dreamlands tales of H. P. Lovecraft.

The love affair soured as Johnson matured, however. The author reveals how, during his university years, he became increasingly disenchanted with fantasy and a great deal of entertainment media in general. Black characters tended to be stereotypical and treated unfairly if they were included at all. "The Vale of the Lost Women" (a notorious Conan story that remained unpublished during Howard's lifetime) and the African adventures of Solomon Kane are cited as being particularly troubling.

Despite a sense of exclusion from fantasy, his interest lingered. Casual online research into Fritz Leiber's Fafhrd and the Gray Mouser eventually led him to discover the late Charles R. Saunders' groundbreaking Maasai-themed hero Imaro, marketed as a "Black Tarzan."

This introduction to the sub-genre Saunders labeled *Sword & Soul* enthralled Johnson, inspiring him to create his own characters and world informed by the Africa of yore. Interactions with other active Sword & Soul creators like Milton J. Davis and P. Djeli Clark further challenged Johnson and influenced his work. His first published short story, "In the Wake of Mist," appeared in 2011's *Griots: A Sword and Soul Anthology*, edited by Davis. Published by Johnson's own freshly-established Far Afield Press in April of 2022, *The Obanaax* collects four further energetic Sword & Soul adventures.

While the protagonists differ for each story, the tales all share a common setting: the continents of Mbor and Gaabar, in the remains of the fallen island empire of Xanjarnou. Given the coastal focus of the included map and the author's own Trinidadian heritage, one might expect the stories to draw upon the culture of the Black diaspora in the Caribbean. Instead, Johnson sticks with a West African-inspired milieu. Whereas Johnson's contemporary Davis adopts a mythologized version of Earth for his Changa tales, Johnson's is a secondary world in which two moons rule the night sky and the spirits of the ancestral dead remain close to their descendants.

While the tribes of the savannahs are derided as unsophisticated yokels by pampered city folk, it is these so-called barbarians and similarly rugged mercenaries who act as the prime movers in the stories collected here.

The novella-length title story "The Obanaax" has as its heroine Wurri, a hardened nomad of the Asuah. She deals with treacherous grave robbers, a cursed bondslave, and otherworldly threats in her quest to reclaim her people's sacred artifact.

"The Oculus of Kii" focuses on barbarian warrior Sangara (who interestingly shares a name with the protagonist of "In the Wake of Mist," from *Griots*). When a wrestling bout gone awry leaves him deeply indebted to his master, he's dispatched on a deadly treasure hunt. Sangara is forced to contend with the spirits of the dead, masked cultists trespassing on their burial grounds, and the cult's unholy patron.

"Cock and Bull," the pinnacle of the book for this reviewer, features tribesman N'Gara, nicknamed "Clean" for his good looks. New to city life, N'Gara finds work as an enforcer for an avaricious merchant. He soon discovers that allegiances can be fluid in the "civilized" world. N'Gara is less of a bumpkin than he appears, however, and possesses an agenda of his own.

The book concludes with "For Wine and Roast," a rousing tale of disparate mercenaries tasked with retrieving their merchant employer's stolen pendant, a trinket of considerable magical might.

The evocative presentation of the setting was the highlight of this book. Johnson conjures a world in which *nguimb*-clad sellswords rub shoulders with rich merchants in silken *mbubb* gowns, drinking sorghum beer from calabash bowls in *daakaa* drinking houses lit by gourd lanterns. Like Michael Moorcock, Johnson is able to give the reader just enough scaffolding to set a scene without overburdening them with excess exposition. The text is also generously spiced with terms from a variety of West African languages like Wolof, Malinke, and Songhay. A glossary is tucked away in the back matter, but usually context clues make the non-English terms' meanings obvious.

The author also excels when his heroes are thrown into armed conflict, particularly with supernatural opponents. The action scenes are frenetic and viscerally described, and Johnson's monsters run the gamut from oozing, tentacled horrors to all-too-solid masses of bulging muscle.

In the introduction, Johnson acknowledges that he is still polishing his craft, and he runs into trouble when his plots become less straightforward. Some of the stories introduce twists late in the game; a seemingly implacable enemy may have a change of heart, or an ally might prove less steadfast than originally thought. At times these sudden developments are not handled as elegantly as they could have been, and some additional foreshadowing or telegraphing could have helped these moments land with more dramatic impact.

For a self-published volume, the prose is largely typo-free, but it would have benefited from another editing pass. Commas occasionally appear in mystifying locations or are conspicuous by their absence.

While this book is a promising debut, one gets the sense that Johnson's best tales lie ahead, as his raw talent is honed by experience. That being said, Sword & Sorcery fans are fortunate that representation in the form of Saunders' Imaro managed to coax this fresh talent back into the fantasy fold. Johnson is an author to watch.

Born in Spain and raised in the United States, Robin Marx (he/him) has lived in Japan for more than two decades. He works in the video game industry, handling localization and international licensing. In addition to over a dozen video games, his writing has appeared in a number of roleplaying game supplements. He lives with his wife and their two daughters.

@RobinMarx

What is New Edge Sword & Sorcery?

Oliver Brackenbury

Hey, thanks for reading our first ever issue! I thought it'd be best you did so before I answer the titular question here, to let you go in without feeling told how to feel about what you'd be seeing. Now then, Mr. Editor, what is this thing you've named the magazine after?

"New Edge Sword & Sorcery" is definitely a work in progress. Though the term was coined by Howard Andrew Jones in the 2000s, as you read earlier, it vanished quickly, only reappearing in April of this year. Barely five months later and you hold this magazine in your very hands! Let's review the tweet-length guiding philosophy from our table of contents:

New Edge Sword & Sorcery takes the genre's virtues of its outsider protagonists, thrilling energy, wondrous weirdness, and a large body of classic tales, then alloys inclusivity, mutual creator support, a positive fan community, and enthusiastic promotion of new works into the mix.

The first half of that list contains major elements of the ninety-plus-year-old literary sub-genre known as "Sword & Sorcery," and the second half contains modern values we believe will help guide the genre back to—even beyond—the mainstream levels of popularity it enjoyed during its second wave of the 1960s through early '80s. That's where the "New Edge" comes in.

All right, so what's regular Sword & Sorcery?

"Sword & Sorcery" is a term for a sub-genre which used to be quite distinct from other fantasy literature, like the high fantasy of *Lord of the Rings*, but which has become diluted since the sub-genre died down to a glowing ember back in the '80s. Now if you say "Sword & Sorcery" to most people, they'll just think of contemporary fantasy in general—anything with a sword or a wizard in it.

The author of my favorite definition, Brian Murphy, has an article on one aspect—outsider protagonists—that you can read in this very magazine. I'd also encourage checking out his book, *Flame & Crimson: A History of Sword-and-Sorcery* for a deeper dive, fascinating literary history, and reading recommendations galore. But here's my crack at a brief definition:

Sword & Sorcery tells short, episodic tales with historical and horror-tinged influences, of outsider protagonists with personal motivations, often facing dark and dangerous magic.

Already, I want to expand, or argue with, this definition! The discussions of such things never truly end, as no definition can encompass every aspect or please every reader. However, I think this helps get across how Sword & Sorcery is more specific than most of us think.

Without any tedious gatekeeping, part of the magazine's mission is to help make people aware of this marvellous sub-genre and its rich history, to help make "Sword & Sorcery" mean what it used to, to the population at large rather than just the dedicated folk who have kept that ember hot during the cold, windy decades between the '80s and now.

We want to help fan that ember back into a roaring flame of mainstream popularity and understanding by giving people a new reason to talk about it, talk that'll draw them in to read these great stories, old and new, and enjoy the dynamic artistic tradition that comes with them. Once more, with feeling: that's where the "New Edge" comes in—a guiding philosophy which can help knock the dirt and verdigris off this sweet, sharp blade we call "Sword & Sorcery."

So why did all this make me excited enough to commit to editing and founding a whole new magazine?

What I Think Is Exciting About New Edge Sword & Sorcery

Well...

It's flexible. There is incredible room to play and experiment within the elastic edges of this genre, something strongly encouraged by the New Edge movement.

Second-wave Sword & Sorcery author Michael Moorcock created one of the greatest S&S protagonists of all time, Elric, by intentionally turning the genre's most famous original character, Conan the Cimmerian, inside out. A mightily strong, magic-fearing, self-assured, bronze-skinned barbarian who would one day become king of the most civilized nation in the land led to an albino emperor dependent on drugs and magic to function, frequently miserable and conflicted, whose own adventures would destroy his kingdom, setting him adrift. Both of these characters fit comfortably within the genre.

In fact Sword & Sorcery was often used like a cloak by Conan's creator, Robert E. Howard, himself, placing it around the shoulders of other genres like pirate stories, the locked-room mystery, and western frontier tales. What other genres might it adorn?

Sword & Sorcery can be a lot of things and still be Sword & Sorcery.

Just think about the incredible variation in automobiles since they were invented. There are cars powered by electricity, cars you can drive into a lake like launching a boat, cars of all shapes and sizes and colors, to say nothing of trucks, buses, RVs etc., but we recognize them all as automobiles.

Sword & Sorcery is a great place for characters from marginalized backgrounds. With its focus on outsider protagonists who succeed because, not in spite, of who they are, I think S&S is ripe for more stories centered on people who haven't had a great deal of representation in popular fiction until quite recently. I'm dying, for example, to read a Sword & Sorcery story with a transgender protagonist.

A chance to take a break from reading, or stand out as an author, from the dominant publishing trend of six-hundred-page-plus fantasy tomes (not that there's anything wrong with them) by reading or crafting swift, short stories, novellas, and novels.

Sword & Sorcery protagonists pretty much always punch up. Though they often are motivated more by greed, glory, or other forms of self-interest, Sword & Sorcery protagonists are forever stealing from, fighting against, and otherwise striking back at the cruel, corrupt people who fancy themselves masters of the universe.

It's almost entirely lacking Chosen One narratives or a "muggle" style device teaching readers, in order to be special, you have to be separate from and

above the rest of us puny humans. On the author side, it's also a very inclusive genre across lines of income and education, welcoming blue collar and blue blood creators alike.

That said, no doubt, in many of the older works you find outdated attitudes regarding race and gender which are best left behind. Luckily you can…

Stand on the shoulders of a long tradition without being chained to it. There's a rich body of work going back to the 1930s pulp magazines, and plenty of already existing fans who'll enthusiastically share titles and authors to check out, as well as how to find them.

Writers can take all kinds of inspiration, and readers can enjoy all kinds of new-to-them stories, while discovering how their influence has affected contemporary works. Writers can also have fun remixing and building on this canon. Like I say above, it's flexible. Meanwhile, if you're a tabletop role-playing gamer, you'll find more inspiration for your games then you'll know what to do with!

And the outdated attitudes you sometimes encounter?

Creators can—and should, in my opinion—just leave those on the cutting room floor, borrowing only the virtues of the old works, like their quick pacing, or lack of restrictions to the imagination such as a Dungeons & Dragons-style codification of the uncanny or publisher stigma against mixing genre elements. Outside of a game with its need for rules & definitions, why would you ever standardize the fantastic? It feels counter-intuitive to me, thus my love of the far less predictable, weird and wonderful fantastic elements you'll find in Sword & Sorcery, past and present.

The way I see it is, we still study, build on, and remix artistic inspiration from the Ancient

Greeks, and we do this without continuing their practice of only letting men participate in the Olympics, trying to predict the future by sacrificing animals, or wiping our butts with flat stones.

Now, if you're already familiar with Sword & Sorcery in general, you might have read all my points and found yourself thinking "What's New Edge about that? It just sounds like Sword & Sorcery."

Well there's the trick, it isn't a huge leap to make if you're already a Sword & Sorcery fan.

The New Edge building to a New Wave

To me, the New Edge difference is a dedication to pushing boundaries through experimentation and inclusiveness, enriching the whole scene with new readers and authors, and an equal focus on creation and promotion of new works, as well as curation and promotion of past ones.

It's that simple.

Add in a community dedicated to uplifting each other, rather than endlessly fighting over how many carbon copy Conans you can fit on the head of a pin, and I think we just might be able to build the already in-progress resurgence of Sword & Sorcery popularity to a big, bold third wave washing across the world's pages and screens!

That's what I believe about New Edge Sword & Sorcery, beliefs which I'm going to be expressing through this magazine, where I hope you'll join me.

That's issue #0!

Thank you so much for reading. This was an unpaid passion project for all involved, sold at no profit to anyone. Imagine what we could do with funding to pay creators, or hire a printer so we can produce something nicer than Amazon Print On Demand!

If enough people show interest, we'll feel confident launching a crowdfunding campaign early in 2023 to fund issues #1 & 2 of the magazine. The most valuable way people can do that is by joining our mailing list – linked to on www.newedgeswordandsorcery.com – as, in the world of crowdfunding, the length of such a list is the best way to measure your chances of success. Sharing the list sign-up is great too.

Naturally we'll also be seeing how many people download the ePub of #0, buy the soft and hardcovers, convince their friendly local bookstore to carry copies of #0, follow us on social media, share pictures of themselves proudly thrusting #0 toward the heavens, and so on and so forth.

I can only hope we've inspired you.

Keep Your Sword Sharp and Your Sorcery Numinous,

Oliver Brackenbury

A Brackenbooks Publication

2022

Made in the USA
Las Vegas, NV
12 April 2024

88559151R00049